"Hey, Lacey!"

Lacey turned around and felt her breath catch in her throat. Kevin Jamison was running toward her, a friendly smile on his handsome face.

"Hi, Kevin," she murmured as he stopped in front of her.

"Great football game, wasn't it?" His face was flushed with excitement, and he was standing so close to her that she could smell the spicy scent of his cologne.

"Yes, it was very exciting," Lacey said, wondering how she was managing to talk to the boy of her dreams without choking.

He looked at her curiously. "You sound sort of funny."

She gestured to her throat and smiled. "I think I yelled too much," she explained. *Just my luck*, Lacey thought to herself. *Kevin finally talks to me, and I sound like I have a frog in my throat!*

Other books in the FIRST KISS series:

FALLING FOR YOU
Carla Bracale

BANTAM BOOKS
TORONTO · NEW YORK · LONDON · SYDNEY · AUCKLAND

All the characters in this book are fictitious and any resemblance to actual persons living or dead is purely coincidental.

With special thanks to Marimekko

FALLING FOR YOU
A BANTAM BOOK 0 553 40089 4

Originally published in U.S.A. by Ballantine Books, a division of Random House, Inc.

Produced by Butterfield Press, Inc.
133 Fifth Avenue
New York, New York 10003

First publication in Great Britain

PRINTING HISTORY
Bantam edition published 1990

Bantam Books are published by Transworld Publishers Ltd., 61–63 Uxbridge Road, Ealing, London W5 5SA, in Australia by Transworld Publishers (Australia) Pty. Ltd., 15–23 Helles Avenue, Moorebank, NSW 2170, and in New Zealand by Transworld Publishers (N.Z.) Ltd., Cnr. Moselle and Waipareira Avenues, Henderson, Auckland.

Printed and bound in Great Britain by
Cox & Wyman Ltd., Reading, Berks.

To my family,
especially Darlene,
my very own Lacey

Chapter 1

If anything could go wrong, it would. Everyone said that was Murphy's Law, but there were times when Lacey Sinclair thought that particular law had been written just for her.

Today was the first day of school . . . the first day she would be attending Oak Ridge High School as a freshman. She had been looking forward to this for as long as she could remember. Finally, she was going to be a high-school student—and suddenly everything was going wrong!

First her normally reliable clock radio had refused to go off at six o'clock. When she opened her eyes at six-thirty, Lacey had been panic stricken that thirty minutes had slipped by. She needed that half hour desperately, to get ready for school. But it figured—the most important day in her life, and she had overslept!

With only a half hour left before the school bus would arrive to pick her up, Lacey flew into action. She showered in exactly seven minutes and got dressed in another four minutes, which left nineteen minutes to work on the most important things of all, her makeup and her hair.

She sat down at her makeup table and stared at her reflection in the mirror. The image that reflected back showed just how excited she was. Her blue eyes sparkled brighter than usual and her cheeks were flushed a pretty shade of pink. *And why shouldn't I be excited?* she asked herself with a smile. *Today is the beginning of a whole new world!* New friends, football games, dances, maybe even a real boyfriend . . . She shivered with nervousness and quickly began applying her makeup.

Her mom had told her last year that when she entered high school she could start to date. The idea of going out with a boy thrilled Lacey, but it also frightened her. She had never spent any time alone with a boy she liked. What would she talk about on a date? Where would she go? Oh, well, if she was lucky, she would be an expert in dating soon!

"There!" she said, putting away her mascara and surveying her reflection. The beige face powder almost managed to cover the pale freckles that dotted her nose, and her blond hair fell in waves across her shoulders. Her eye makeup made her pale eyelashes look long and thick, and the pink eye shadow matched the rose-colored sweater dress she was wearing.

"Oh, no!" she murmured as her nose began to itch and her eyes began to water. Surely she wasn't going to sneeze, not now! "Ah-choo!" Lacey looked back at her reflection and groaned. Her mascara had created perfect dark rings around her eyes, making her look like a raccoon. Lacey's Law. Something could have gone wrong, and it did. She frantically grabbed a jar of makeup remover from her bureau and set to repairing the damage from the sneeze.

As Lacey stood at the bus stop, the sun was just awakening, peeking shyly up in the eastern sky, and the air had the distinctive scent of early autumn. The leaves on the trees had already begun to change from the brilliant greens of summer to the muted golds and oranges of fall. But Lacey didn't have time to appreciate the beauty of nature—she was too busy trying to look calm and cool in case the bus came around the corner.

She nervously smoothed down the length of her hair, then straightened an imaginary wrinkle from her dress. She wondered if all the kids in the freshman class were as nervous as she was this morning. Did everyone have butterflies doing acrobatics in the pit of their stomach? She smiled as she thought of Peg, her best friend. Peggy Simmons would never, ever, have butterflies in her stomach. Peg was never nervous or afraid of making a fool of herself. But then, Peg didn't have to live with the bad luck of Lacey's Law. Things didn't go wrong for Peg. Lacey's Law seemed only to apply to Lacey Sinclair.

Last year had been a nightmare of accidents designed to make her life miserable. She'd gotten a severe case of laryngitis the day before the auditions for the big school play. The entire seat of her slacks had ripped while acting the part of Juliet before her English class, and she had fainted during biology while attempting to dissect a frog.

"But no more," she said firmly to herself.

Things would be different for her this year. Surely her run of bad luck was over!

"Please . . . please let this year be great," she whispered fervently as the big yellow school bus rounded the corner and groaned to a halt before her.

"Lacey! Lacey, back here!"

Lacey immediately spotted Peg sitting near the back of the bus and made her way toward her friend.

Peg's dark eyes sparkled as she scooted over to make room for Lacey on the narrow bus seat. "Well, we finally made it to the big time—high school!" Peg grinned broadly, flipping open a notebook and handing it to Lacey.

"What's this?" Lacey scanned the page, as usual finding Peg's handwriting almost impossible to read. "Peg, how are you ever going to get through high school? Your teachers will never be able to read your papers."

"I'll type all the important papers," Peg answered flippantly, grabbing the notebook from Lacey with a sigh of impatience. "This is a list of the clubs we should join and the things we should try out for," Peg explained. "There's the Drama Club, the Glee Club, and, of course, the Pep Club. John says everyone who's anyone belongs to these clubs." John was Peg's older brother, a handsome, well-liked junior. "Then we really should try out for freshman cheerleader, and there's the school play at the end of the year—"

"Hold it, hold it!" Lacey laughed at her friend's elaborate plans. "Slow down. I'm just concentrating on making it through today without any major mishaps." She shook her head and grinned at her best friend. "We haven't even made it through one hour of school yet, and you already have us joining a dozen clubs and trying out for cheerleader!"

"But, Lacey, this stuff is really important. We have to think about our future at Oak Ridge," Peg protested, flipping to the next page in her notebook. "Look, I've even started a list of potential boyfriends."

Lacey giggled as she read the name at the top of the list. "Jon Bon Jovi?"

Peg grinned. "I just put him on the list for fun, but the rest of the names are guys from high school. I looked in John's yearbook and copied down the names of all the major hunks."

"Have you already made your wedding plans, too?" Lacey teased.

"Not yet, but I'll keep you in mind for my maid of honor," Peg quipped. "Lacey, I just want this year to be the best! I mean, we aren't kids anymore, we're in high school."

"Well, right now I'm just hoping I can make it through the day without locking myself in my locker," Lacey reminded her friend.

"You'll do fine," Peg assured her just as the bus came to a screeching halt in front of the three-story brick high school.

Because Oak Ridge High School incorporated the students from three area junior high schools, Lacey didn't recognize most of the students she saw on her way to homeroom. And even the familiar faces, students she had gone to school with last year, looked different, older somehow. As she made her way down the crowded corridor, students she knew smiled at her or waved in silent greeting.

This isn't so bad, she thought. Many of the faces were different, and the school was much bigger than junior high, but it smelled exactly the same: a musty combination of new chalk and old floor wax. The atmosphere was just as noisy and chaotic. She grinned confidently as she opened the door to her homeroom. Yes, it was going to be a great year!

Fourth period, Lacey was racing toward the stairs that led from the third floor to the second floor for her psychology class. She was juggling an armload of books and trying to remember exactly which classroom she was supposed to go to when she saw him.

Standing at a locker near the stairs, he was talking with another boy, and for a second Lacey stopped dead in her tracks and stared. He was not the most handsome guy Lacey had ever seen, but there was something about him that made her heart do flip-flops in her chest. Maybe it was the way his dark hair curled down to his neck, or maybe it was because his brown eyes looked like melted pools of chocolate. It could have been the way that his smile started at one corner of his mouth, then slowly developed into a full grin that lit up his entire face. Whatever it was, Lacey could have stood in the hallway and looked at him forever, but just then he seemed to sense that somebody was staring at him. He looked around and suddenly his gaze met Lacey's.

A blush swept over Lacey's face as she quickly turned away, embarrassed that he'd caught her staring at him. Heading down the stairs, she was grateful when she reached the bottom of the staircase, remembering when their eyes had met. He was so nice-looking, and his smile had made her feel so . . . funny.

The bell rang, and she was now officially late for class. She hurried down the deserted hall and paused at the door of the classroom, reluctant to make a spectacle of herself by going in late.

Finally, realizing she couldn't stand in the hallway forever, she squared her shoulders and entered the classroom, blushing furiously.

Lacey felt the eyes of every single person in the classroom focus on her. She turned her attention to the teacher, a thin, dark-haired man with horn-rimmed glasses and a thick moustache.

"Ah, Miss Lacey Sinclair, I presume?" His bushy eyebrows shot up quizzically.

Lacey nodded, wishing that the floor beneath her would open up and swallow her whole.

"Perhaps you would like to take a seat. Or do you prefer to monitor the class from your present position?"

Lacey nodded a quick yes, then shook her head, no. She was so embarrassed! Spying an empty seat in the third row, she hurried toward it, keeping her eyes focused firmly on the empty seat and away from the faces of her fellow classmates.

She had just about made it to the desk when her foot hooked on the bottom of the chairs, making her suddenly pitch forward. She caught her balance, but not before the stack of books in her arms flew forward as if with a life of their own.

Whooomph!

Lacey could tell by the sound that her books had landed on someone's stomach. She looked up nervously and couldn't believe her eyes. Her books were sitting on the lap of the boy she had seen only moments before at the top of the stairs.

Let me die! she thought as she mumbled an apology. She took her books from him and sank down in the empty seat directly behind him. How had he gotten to class before her? she wondered. She stared at the back of his head, knowing if she looked around she would probably either burst into hysterical giggles or break down and cry from the humiliation.

Lacey closed her eyes for a moment and started to imagine what her entrance into the classroom could have been like.

In her mind she saw herself floating into the classroom, walking as gracefully as a ballerina. "Excuse me," she'd say with just the right amount of humility and politeness. "I'm terribly sorry I'm late. My name is Lacey Sinclair."

"That's quite all right. On the first day of school it's difficult to find your way around." The teacher would smile at her. "Please, Miss Sinclair, have a seat."

Lacey would nod graciously and move toward the empty seat in the third row. As she walked, oh, so gracefully, oh, so beautifully, the boy with the chocolate-colored eyes would gaze at her with open interest and admiration. A small smile lifted Lacey's lips.

Lacey's daydream was interrupted when the teacher began passing out textbooks. It was just her luck: her first big chance to impress the guy and she'd tripped at his feet and thrown her books in his lap!

"Lacey! Wait up!" Peg called as Lacey turned down the hall, away from the classroom.

Lacey turned and waited for her friend to catch up.

"Gosh, Lacey, weren't you mortified?" Peg asked as she fell into step next to Lacey. "I would have died! You looked so funny when your books landed on Kevin Jamison."

"Kevin Jamison?" Lacey looked at Peg with interest, walking down the hall toward the lunchroom. So, the boy with the chocolate eyes had a nice name, too. She smiled and pushed open the door to the cafeteria. But her smile faded as she gazed around the noisy crowded room.

"Wow! This is great!" Peg said enthusiastically, grabbing one of the plastic trays and heading for the salad bar.

This isn't great, it's scary, Lacey thought, looking around in awe. She walked through the line in a daze, then paid the cashier for her lunch. She stood motionless, holding her tray and staring out at the huge lunchroom filled with other students.

Lacey had never seen so many kids in one place in her life. How would they ever find empty seats?

"Lacey, over here!" Peg called from a long table.

Gratefully, Lacey hurried over and slid into the seat across from Peg.

"Don't look now, but your friend Kevin Jamison just came into the cafeteria," Peg remarked, staring over Lacey's shoulder.

"He's not my friend," Lacey replied, nervously taking a big bite of her hot dog.

"Well, he's coming this way and he's looking right at you!" Peg said excitedly.

The hot dog in Lacey's mouth suddenly felt like—and tasted like—a big piece of cotton. She managed to swallow just as she felt a hesitant tap on her shoulder.

"Uh . . . Lacey Sinclair, right?" Kevin asked, smiling at her.

Lacey stared at him in silence, then gasped as Peg kicked her sharply under the table. "Yes . . . I'm Lacey." Was that really her voice that spoke, that whispery voice that sounded like something was wrong with her vocal cords?

Kevin hesitated, then smiled again, the crooked, cute smile that made Lacey's heart thud so loudly she was certain everyone in the cafeteria could hear it. "You aren't going to throw any more books at me, are you?"

"Oh, no." Lacey blushed. "I'm really sorry about that."

"Don't worry about it. But when you gathered up your books, you missed one." He held up one of her English books.

"Thanks." Lacey smiled shyly, as she took the book and carefully put it next to her tray.

"Well, I'd better be going," he said, then turned and walked away.

Lacey smiled at Peg. "I talked to him, and I didn't say anything stupid or do anything stupid!"

Peg shook her head, her forehead creased with concern. "Yeah, but you've got the grossest glob of mustard on your chin and it was there the whole time you were talking to him."

"No!" Lacey grabbed for her napkin and wiped her face. Sure enough, she'd had yellow mustard on her chin. "I can't believe it."

"It's no big deal. Everyone gets food on their face sometimes," Peg said, attempting to make her friend feel better.

"The one time I get a chance to talk to the boy of my dreams, and I have mustard dripping off my chin. How gross!" Lacey said glumly, shoving her lunch tray away.

"Oh, so you do like him, don't you?" Peg asked eagerly.

"What difference does it make? He'll never like me. First I trip and throw my books at him; then I talk to him with mustard on my face. Talk about bad luck!" Lacey sighed.

"Lacey, if you really like him, then what you need is a plan," Peg said enthusiastically. "Come over tonight and we'll make a list of things you can do and say to make Kevin like you."

Despite her unhappiness, Lacey laughed, knowing how much Peg loved to make lists. Sometimes she wondered if Peg made lists of lists! "Okay, I'll come over tonight after supper."

Both girls jumped as the bell rang. Peg stood up and put her books under one arm, balancing her tray with the other. "I have to get to biology, but I'll see you later. Oh, this is so exciting, Lacey. Only the first day of school and you've already found your dream guy!" With a wave, Peg hurried to put her tray on the conveyor belt to the dish room.

Sure, I've found my dream guy, Lacey thought as she walked toward her next class. The question was, would he ever like her?

Chapter 2

"So, how did the rest of your day go?" Peg asked the minute Lacey settled in the bus seat next to her after school.

"Okay. How about yours?" Lacey looked at Peg curiously.

Peg frowned. "I'm sort of disappointed in high school."

"Why?" Lacey stared at her friend.

"Well, one thing that doesn't change in high school is that all the teachers still expect you to do a ton of homework." She made a face that looked as if she had bitten into a sour lemon. "I probably have two hours of homework to do tonight, and today is only the first day of school!"

Lacey laughed. "Somehow we'll manage to

get through all the homework this year, just like we did last year."

"I was sort of hoping that homework would be against the law in high school," Peg moaned, shifting the large stack of books on her lap.

"Fat chance!" Lacey giggled as the school bus began to move out of the school parking lot.

"Did you see you-know-who anymore today?" Peg asked, leaning closer to Lacey so their conversation wouldn't be overheard.

Lacey shook her head. "No. What about you? Did you see any of the hunks you have on your potential boyfriend list?"

Peg's oval face lit up. "Josh Alton is in my speech class, and I've put a big star next to his name on my list."

"Josh Alton? I don't think I know who he is," Lacey said, her forehead wrinkled in thought.

Peg leaned even closer to Lacey. "Oh, Lacey, he's gorgeous! He's a sophomore and he has beautiful blond hair and crystal blue eyes to die for!"

Lacey smiled at Peg, secretly thinking that Josh didn't sound any dreamier than Kevin. Still, she was happy Peg had found somebody she was interested in, too. "Did you get a chance to talk to him or anything?" she asked.

"Not today, but tomorrow I'm going to make sure I get a chance." She looked at Lacey and giggled. "I could always use your trick and trip and fall on him!"

"I didn't do that on purpose!" Lacey protested, vividly remembering the humiliation she had felt when she had tossed her textbooks into Kevin's stomach. She looked at her friend with admiration. Peg would think nothing of walking right up to Josh Alton and starting a conversation. Peg would know exactly what to say to capture Josh's attention. Lacey couldn't imagine doing that with Kevin—she had no idea what she would say. "Peg, doesn't the thought of talking to Josh make you sort of nervous?" she asked hesitantly.

"Not really." Peg shrugged. "I want to get to know him, and the only way to do that is to talk to him!"

Lacey wondered if perhaps there wasn't something wrong with her. Peg made it all sound so easy. She wasn't scared by the prospect of talking to a boy she liked. So why did the thought of talking to Kevin make Lacey feel as if her stomach were tying itself in knots? Did other girls her age feel like talking to a guy was no big deal? *Maybe I'm just weird,* Lacey thought to herself, biting her bottom lip.

"Whoops! This is me!" Peg exclaimed as

the bus came to a stop and the door opened. "Don't forget, tonight after supper at my house. We'll make plans for you-know-who!" she yelled over her shoulder as she stepped off the bus.

Lacey laughed and made an okay sign with her fingers to Peg through the glass of the bus window. Peg waved back in agreement.

Minutes later Lacey got off the bus and walked across the street to the small, two-bedroom ranch house where she and her mother had lived for the past five years.

"Mom, I'm home!" Lacey called out as she dumped her school books into the big living room chair.

"In the kitchen, honey," her mom's voice rang out.

Lacey found her mother sitting at the kitchen table, the newspaper and a cup of coffee in front of her.

"How's my favorite high-school freshman?" Wanda Sinclair smiled brightly at Lacey.

"Okay." Lacey sat down in the kitchen chair across from her mom. "How are you?"

"Tired," her mom admitted. "The emergency room was a real madhouse last night. I was just getting into bed when I heard your alarm go off this morning."

Lacey smiled at her mom sympathetically. "Maybe you can get in an early night tonight. Aren't you off tonight?"

Her mom nodded, then smiled. "How about a cup of hot cocoa and some girl talk?" she asked cheerfully, getting up to make a saucepan of hot cocoa. "What do you think of your classes? Do you like all of your teachers?"

"The classes should be all right. Peg is already complaining about all the homework, though."

Mrs. Sinclair laughed. "If I know Peg, it won't be long before she'll have a list of the easiest ways to save time while doing homework."

Lacey joined in her mother's laughter. "She's already made a list of all the clubs to join to make her superpopular, and she'll do it, too!"

Wanda poured her daughter a cup of the warmed, hot cocoa, then poured herself some more coffee and rejoined Lacey at the table. "That's one thing I can say about Peg, she's never been afraid to try new things." Wanda paused a moment to take a sip of her coffee, then continued. "And what about you? Do you have a master plan for being superpopular?"

"Not me. I just want to get through this

year without doing too many dumb things,"
Lacey explained to her mom. She took a sip
of her hot cocoa and licked the chocolate
moustache off her upper lip.

"Don't tell me you're still worried about
that Lacey's Law nonsense!" Wanda frowned
at her daughter. "Honey, everyone goes
through stages of bad luck at one time or
another."

"Yeah, but not like me. I've got the worst
luck in the whole wide world." Lacey
propped her elbows on the table and rested
her chin in her hands. "Sometimes I feel
like if I entered a contest, and I was the only
person in the world who entered that contest, I'd still lose!"

Lacey's mom laughed and ran a hand
through her curly blond hair. "Honey, you
take everything too seriously. You have to
learn to laugh when you have a streak of
bad luck." Lacey's mom stood up and kissed
Lacey on the top of her head. "I'm going to
take a quick shower, and if you have a lot of
homework, you'd better hit the books!"

Lacey nodded, watching as her mom left
the kitchen and disappeared into the bathroom. She thought about her mother's
words, then thought about having that glob
of mustard on her chin while talking to
Kevin. Her mom just didn't understand.

There was no way Lacey would ever be able to laugh at that particular incident!

She got up from the table and quickly rinsed her cocoa mug in the sink, then went back into the living room, grabbed her school books, and headed for her bedroom.

As always, the first thing Lacey saw in her room was the framed picture of her father that sat on the nightstand next to her bed. She sank down on the bed, setting her school books to the side, then picked up the picture of her father. Lacey's memories of her dad were distant and fuzzy. She had been ten years old when he died, and with each day that passed her memories of him grew dimmer and dimmer. She felt guilty sometimes because she didn't remember him more clearly. But, logically, she knew that part of the reason she had fuzzy memories of him was that her father had traveled frequently and had rarely been at home.

Her heart felt the funny sort of emptiness it always felt whenever she looked at his picture. Oh, he'd been so handsome, and so tall. He always came home from his business trips with a suitcase full of presents for his daughter. Then one day he hadn't come home, and her mother had told her there had been a plane crash. And Lacey's life had changed forever.

Sometimes Lacey believed that plane crash had been the beginning of her bad luck. She often wondered what her life would be like now if her father hadn't gotten on that particular plane. Why couldn't he have taken another flight on another day? She carefully placed her father's picture back on the nightstand with a deep sigh. Bad luck . . . it was the story of her life!

She lay back on her bed and opened up the book Kevin had returned to her at lunchtime. For a moment she stared at the first page blankly, remembering the way Kevin had looked as he had spoken to her. She smiled softly to herself as she thought of the way his warm smile lit up his entire face. He was so wonderful! She hugged the book tightly against her chest and thought about Kevin's gorgeous brown eyes. Then she reluctantly turned to the first chapter in the book. She had to get her homework done if she wanted to go to Peg's house that evening. And she had to talk to Peg if she ever wanted to get Kevin to like her! For once, homework was worth doing.

It was nearly an hour later when Lacey's mother knocked on the door. "Lacey, may I come in?"

"Sure," Lacey replied. She closed her

algebra book, relieved that she had finished her homework.

"Bill just called and he invited us out to supper tonight," her mom explained, smiling at Lacey. "He wants to take us to that new Italian restaurant at the mall. I told him how much you love Italian food."

"Oh, mom, do I have to go?" Lacey sat up and looked at her mother unhappily. "I've already made plans to go over to Peg's house this evening. We have a . . . er . . . a project we're working on together."

The smile on Mrs. Sinclair's face slowly faded. "Honey, couldn't you work with Peg some other night, and go with us? Bill would really like an opportunity to get to know you better."

"I'm sorry. Tonight just isn't a good night. I *have* to go to Peg's. How about some other night?" Lacey asked.

"Okay, we'll make it another night," her mom agreed softly, leaving Lacey's room and closing the door behind her.

The minute the door closed, Lacey's smile turned into a deep frown. Her mom had been dating Bill for the last month, but Lacey had absolutely no desire to get to know Bill better. She'd only met him twice, but that had been more than enough. Why was her mother dating him, anyway? Bill

was a short man, with thinning dark hair
and glasses. Her mother had never felt the
need to date anyone before. Why now? And
why Bill?

Lacey's eyes narrowed slightly as she once
again picked up the picture of her father.
Her mother might be forgetting about the
tall, golden-haired giant who had been a
part of their lives, but Lacey would never
forget him . . . never!

Chapter 3

It was nearly seven o'clock by the time Lacey got to Peg's house. After saying a quick hello to Mrs. Simmons, Lacey ran up the stairs and knocked rapidly on Peg's closed bedroom door.

"Come on in," a muffled voice called out. Lacey opened the door and immediately spotted Peg stretched out across her perfectly made bed.

"What are you doing?" Lacey asked, sitting down on the bed beside Peg and surveying her bedroom. It never failed to amaze her that Peg kept her room so neat that it looked like something out of a designer magazine. There was a place for everything and everything was in its place. In contrast,

Lacey's room always looked like the "after" picture of a natural disaster!

"Yuk! Finishing up some algebra homework. I hate math!" Peg said passionately, slamming her textbook shut.

"Me, too," Lacey agreed. "How many times in my life am I going to need to know what x equals?"

"Beats me. That same thought applies to a lot of the junk they make us learn in school." Peg rolled over on her back, her brown eyes staring up at the bedroom ceiling as she continued. "When will I ever need to know the proper, scientific names for the various parts of a plant?"

Lacey giggled and flopped over on her back. "Or who was the president of the United States in 1877?"

"Or what did Shakespeare say in his stupid plays?" Peg added.

"It would be a lot better if the schools taught us important stuff," Lacey said seriously. "You know, like how to get a good summer job or how to make an allowance last through a week."

"Or how to get the best seats at a Bon Jovi concert, or how to get a date with the boy of your dreams. Which reminds me . . ." Peg sat up and grabbed a magazine off the bedside table. "There's a big article in here about crushes. Remember last year how you felt about Michael J. Fox, how you went to see *Back to the Future* ten times, and how you collected all his pictures and everything?"

Lacey blushed. "Don't remind me," she murmured, conscious of how childish she had been.

"This article says that was normal, but now that you're a teenager, it's time to move on to somebody more accessible. Somebody like Kevin Jamison, for instance." Peg leaned over and picked up the notebook that lay on the floor next to the bed. She flipped through it eagerly. "Wait until you hear all the things I found out for you about him!"

"What? Tell me everything!" Lacey quickly sat up and tried to get a look inside Peg's notebook.

"Ah, here it is!" Peg pronounced triumphantly. She held the notebook up in front of her, carefully keeping the page hidden from Lacey's eager eyes. "Okay, here we go. First, Kevin Jamison is a junior at Oak Ridge High School—"

"I know he's a junior and where he goes to school. Now tell me something I don't know!" Lacey exclaimed impatiently, her heart beating wildly in her chest.

"Okay, okay. Hold your horses." Peg giggled once again, holding the notebook up in the air as Lacey tried to grab it out of her hands.

"Come on, Peg, you've got a whole page written there. What else do you know about Kevin?" Lacey settled back on the bed and looked at her best friend.

"Okay," Peg relented, sensing how important this was to her friend. "Kevin Jamison loves sports, all kinds of sports. He plays varsity basketball and last summer he helped coach a little-league baseball team."

Lacey nodded, urging her friend to continue.

"He loves pepperoni pizza and anything barbequed. He has a little brother named Billy and his favorite color is blue," Peg concluded. "Oh, yeah, he really likes Van Halen, too."

"How did you ever manage to find all that out?"

"Easy." Peg shrugged her slender shoulders. "John and Kevin are good friends."

"You asked your brother about Kevin?" Lacey shrieked. "What on earth did you say to him?"

Peg shrugged once again. "I just told John that you're sort of interested in Kevin and wanted to know a little bit about him. It was nothing."

"Nothing?" Lacey slapped her hand across her forehead with a loud moan and fell backward on the bed. "Peg, how could you do this to me?"

"How could I do what to you?" Peg looked at Lacey innocently.

Lacey sat back up and glared at Peg. "How could you tell John that I'm interested in Kevin? I'm so embarrassed!"

"John didn't think anything about it," Peg claimed, shrugging.

"What if he says something to Kevin?" Lacey asked, horrified. "What if John tells Kevin I wanted to know all about him, that I'm interested in him?" Lacey flopped back on the bed once again. "I'll just die if he does that." She jumped back up and grabbed Peg firmly by the shoulders. "Peg, promise me you'll talk to John and tell him not to say anything to Kevin." Lacey shook Peg by the shoulders. "Promise me!"

"Okay, okay, but if you don't cut it out you'll shake out all my teeth and I won't be able to talk to anyone." Peg grinned impishly. "Then I'll look just like old Mrs. Windslow."

Lacey giggled and released Peg's shoulders, thinking of Mrs. Windslow, the eighth-grade math teacher who wore false teeth. She sobered and looked at Peg seriously. "But, you do promise you'll talk to John for me."

"I most solemnly do swear," Peg pledged, raising her right hand as if she were taking an oath.

Lacey nodded, satisfied that Peg would keep the promise. She picked up Peg's notebook and looked at the page with all the information about Kevin. Although she could hardly read Peg's scrawled handwriting, she remembered every single word Peg had read to her. She wasn't surprised that Kevin was involved in sports; he had the physical build of a guy who was sports-minded. He was tall and slender, but he had wide shoulders.

He liked pepperoni pizza and anything barbequed. Although Lacey's personal favorite kind of pizza was mushroom, she, too, loved barbeque. Blue was his favorite color. Her forehead wrinkled as she tried to remember her wardrobe at home and all the blue clothes she owned. Lacey had never really liked the music of Van Halen, but if that was what Kevin liked, then she would learn to like it, too!

"You have an incredibly dopey look on

your face," Peg said, interrupting Lacey's thoughts. "You must be thinking about Kevin again."

"I am," Lacey confessed with a pink blush on her face. "Look, now that I have all this information about Kevin, what do I do with it? How will it help me get a date with him?" Lacey looked at Peg, feeling helpless.

"Well, the first thing you have to do is talk to him—strike up a conversation. You know, show him you're interested in the same things he is."

"But I don't know anything about sports," Lacey protested.

Peg looked at her patiently. "Lacey, you don't need to know a lot. There are tons of football games on TV every Sunday. Just watch a few and find out who wins. Then on Monday, when you see Kevin, you casually say something like: 'How about those Jets?' Or: 'Aren't those Rams awesome?' Believe me, you get a guy started talking about sports and then all you'll have to do is nod occasionally and smile."

"You always make everything sound so easy," Lacey said.

"And you always make everything seem so hard," Peg countered with a grin. "I think that's why we've been friends for so long. You're always so pessimistic."

"And you're always so optimistic!" Lacey finished, and they grinned at each other.

"Hey, I just thought of something. . . ." Peg scrambled off the bed and disappeared down the hallway before Lacey could ask her what she was doing.

Lacey got up off the bed and wandered around the room restlessly, waiting for Peg to return. It seemed so strange that a boy she knew so little about, had seen only for an hour or so that day, was so important to her. Up until today, Lacey hadn't been very interested in any one boy. Sure, she had dreamed about finding and dating the guy who would be special to her. But up until now no one had really caught her eye. Now there was Kevin. Kevin, with the beautiful chocolate-brown eyes and slow, wonderful smile.

She closed her eyes, easily picturing Kevin's face in her mind. She let her imagination go one step further, envisioning the two of them together at a school dance. She would be dressed in a filmy blue dress that would make her look like a princess, and Kevin would be handsome in a dark blue suit. The school gym would be decorated to look like something straight out of a fairy tale, and the band would be playing soft, romantic music. Kevin would smile softly at her and take her in his arms, and together they would glide across the polished dance floor.

Lacey smiled dreamily, and with her eyes still closed, she began to dance across Peg's bedroom floor, caught up in her wonderful fantasy.

"May I cut in?"

Lacey squealed as a hand fell on her shoulder. Her eyes flew open, a sheepish expression crossing her face as Peg collapsed on the floor, laughing wildly.

"It isn't that funny!" Lacey said crossly, embarrassed at having been caught acting so silly.

"But it was," Peg gasped, tears filling her eyes as she continued howling with laughter. "You had such a goofy look on your face, and your arms were raised like you were dancing with the Invisible Man."

Despite her embarrassment, Lacey giggled. Peg's laughter was contagious, and within seconds both of them were rolling on the floor, their loud laughter echoing off the walls of the bedroom. It took several minutes before they could collect themselves and talk without giggling.

"Where'd you go?" Lacey asked, panting to catch her breath.

"I went to get this." Peg threw Lacey a T-shirt she had wadded up in one hand. "I knew John had one, but it took me a few minutes to find it."

"What is it?" Lacey asked curiously, unwrapping the pale blue shirt. The Van Halen logo was printed on the front of the shirt in big, bold, black letters.

"I figure that ought to be a great conversation starter with Kevin. After all, it's his favorite color and has the name of his favorite group on the front. Wear it to school tomorrow."

"Thanks, Peg." Lacey smiled at her friend. "Are you sure John won't mind if I borrow it?"

"Nah. He probably doesn't even remember he owns it. Besides, John likes you, and I'm sure he wouldn't mind contributing his T-shirt to the 'Get Kevin and Lacey Together' Project!"

"I still wish you hadn't told him that I'm interested in Kevin," Lacey grumbled.

"If I know John, he probably didn't even pay attention when I told him why I wanted to know about Kevin," Peg assured Lacey.

Both girls turned as a knock sounded on Peg's bedroom door. Peg's brother opened the door and stuck his head in. "Can I come in for a minute?" he asked with a small grin.

"What do you want?" Peg demanded.

"I was just wondering if you guys had come up with any surefire ways to get Kevin to ask Lacey out." He looked at Lacey and winked.

"John, you creep, get out of here!" Peg yelled. She picked up a pillow from the bed and threw it at him.

John sidestepped the pillow with a burst of laughter. "Oh, Kevin, Kevin, I love you!" he said in a high-pitched voice.

Lacey felt her face turn bright red. "John, please . . . please don't say anything to him," she pleaded.

"Why shouldn't I?" John asked, his dark eyes twinkling mischievously.

"Because if you don't agree to keep your mouth shut, Lacey and I are going to beat you up!" Peg threatened.

John opened his eyes wide in mock terror. "Oh, I'm *so* scared." He grinned at the two girls, showing that he didn't take seriously his sister's threat of bodily harm.

"Come on, Lacey, let's get him!" Without warning, Peg jumped up from the floor and quickly tackled her brother, who was caught unprepared and landed flat on his back. "Tickle him, Lacey!" Peg squealed, trying to hold her brother down.

Lacey giggled as she approached John, her fingers poised in a tickling position.

"No, Lacey, no tickling," John protested gruffly. "Come on, I mean it," he continued, as Lacey came closer to him.

It was common knowledge that John Simmons hated to be tickled, and Peg and Lacey had often used it to their advantage.

"Lacey, I'm not kidding. Tickling isn't fair!" John struggled to get up, but laughing had made him weak and Peg still had a firm hold on him.

"All's fair in love and war," Lacey replied. "Now, are you going to promise not to tell Kevin?" she asked, her fingers poised just above his stomach.

John's laughter was bringing tears to his eyes, and Peg was giggling nearly as hard as her brother. "Yes, all right, I promise!" John gasped hysterically.

"I don't know, Peg. Do you think we should believe him?" Lacey asked with a wide grin.

"Yeah, but let's tickle him anyway!" Peg shouted.

Darkness was just beginning to fall as Lacey left Peg's house and started walking home. The rule between Lacey and her mother was that Lacey was to be home on weeknights by nine o'clock in the evening. Even though lots of nights her mom wasn't home by then, Lacey still obeyed the rule. She knew her mother's trust was important to her.

When she got to the house, the first thing Lacey did was throw John's T-shirt into the washing machine. The shirt was all wrinkled and smelled vaguely like men's deodorant. She wanted it to be clean and fresh so she could wear it to school in the morning.

It was nearly ten o'clock when she hung the freshly laundered T-shirt on a hanger, stacked her school books on the kitchen table, then went into her room to get ready for bed.

Lacey sat down at her vanity table and began removing her makeup. Once her face was clean, she stared at her reflection in the mirror, wondering if a boy—Kevin, in particular—would really find her pretty.

Her father had always called her his "pretty princess," but Lacey was smart enough to know that most fathers thought their daughters were beautiful, no matter what they looked like.

Lacey knew she wasn't beautiful, but she also knew that most people considered her fairly attractive. Her face was heart-shaped and she had a slight cleft in her chin. She had exactly six freckles scattered across the bridge of her nose that she usually hid beneath makeup. Her long, blond hair was probably her nicest feature. Lacey examined her reflection carefully, wondering if "pretty" was enough to capture Kevin's interest. She could only hope so!

She crawled into bed and turned off her bedside lamp. It was strange that her mother and Bill hadn't shown up yet. How long could it take for two people to eat dinner? Surely her mother didn't seriously like Bill! She turned over on her back and stared up at the ceiling. Then why wasn't her mother home yet?

Chapter 4

Lacey awoke extra early the next morning. She bounded out of bed and right into the shower, anxious for the day to begin. Today was the day she was going to make Kevin notice her.

She took more time than usual getting ready for school, wanting to make sure she looked her absolute best. She put on John's T-shirt and a new pair of stone-washed jeans that hugged her long legs, then carefully applied her makeup and brushed her hair until it was perfect. When she was completely finished she stood and looked at herself in the mirror, satisfied that she looked as good as possible.

Apparently the extra time she had spent on her appearance paid off, for the first thing Peg said when she got on the bus was that Lacey looked great.

"Thanks. Let's just hope this T-shirt does the trick and Keven starts up a conversation with me," Lacey said, nervously smoothing down the front of the shirt.

"Even if he doesn't, it wouldn't hurt if you said something to him first. You know, Lacey, what you need is a class in flirting," Peg said seriously. "Maybe tonight I'll make a list of ways that girls flirt with guys. You can study it and learn how to flirt."

"Please, enough with your lists." Lacey laughed.

"Okay, but when I'm going steady with Josh Alton and you still haven't gotten Kevin to even *talk* to you, don't come running to me for tips on flirting!" Peg exclaimed.

"I promise I won't." Lacey laughed again. "Besides, I'm really not the flirting type of girl. Knowing my luck, I'd try to bat my eyelashes and they would all fall out!"

"Oh, Lacey, you make me so mad sometimes," Peg huffed with exasperation. "You're always down on yourself. I swear, it's no wonder things go wrong for you. Haven't you ever heard the old saying, 'You get what you expect out of life'?"

"That sounds like something out of a stupid fortune cookie," Lacey scoffed.

"It *was* out of a fortune cookie," Peg confessed with a small giggle. "But that doesn't mean it's not true. If you expect things to go wrong, they will. If you expect everything to be great, it will be great!"

"What are you, my own personal cheerleader?" Lacey asked, eyeing Peg suspiciously.

"Well, you need one," Peg replied flippantly. "Anyway, enough of this. The Drama Club is holding its first meeting today after school. You're going to go with me, aren't you?"

"Oh, I don't know, Peg," Lacey hedged. "I'm no good in dramatics. I could never get up onstage and perform before an audience."

"Silly." Peg punched Lacey's shoulder teasingly. "Just because you join the Drama Club doesn't mean you have to be in a play. There are all kinds of other things you can do, like scenery, costumes, and props— don't tell me you can't do any of those things!" Peg lowered her voice to a soft whisper. "Come on, Lacey, we've always done everything together. Besides, the Drama Club is one of the most popular clubs.

We'll meet a lot of people." Peg glanced around the bus. "Who knows? Maybe Kevin will be there," she whispered.

"Okay, okay. You've convinced me." Lacey grinned at her friend. "If we stay for the meeting, how are we going to get home? My mom is working today."

"My mother said she would pick us up," Peg answered as the school bus pulled up before the school and its doors opened. "We can talk about it some more at lunch," Peg exclaimed as the two girls stood up and began to move toward the front door of the bus. "Good luck with Kevin today," she whispered once they stepped off the bus.

"Thanks," Lacey grinned. "I just hope he notices the shirt!"

Waving good-bye, Lacey hurried toward her first-period gym class.

"Okay, ladies!" Mrs. Mulroney, the gym teacher, yelled. "You have only ten minutes before second period, so hit the showers!"

This was the part of gym class that Lacey hated the most. It seemed so horrible to get naked in front of a bunch of girls she hardly knew. Along with the rest of the girls in the class, Lacey quickly stripped off her gym clothes and underwear, then self-consciously ran toward the large, concrete shower where four shower nozzles extended out of the tiled wall. As she waited her turn, she noticed that most of the other girls barely got wet, and almost none of them got any water on their hair. When her turn came, Lacey carefully stepped across the slippery floor. *The trick is to move really fast through the water,* she thought as she approached the first nozzle.

"Hey! Hurry up!" an impatient voice called from behind Lacey.

Taking a deep breath, Lacey scurried past the first shower head, pleased when the warm water just barely misted her skin. Feeling more confident, she ran through the next three shower-nozzle sprays and was hurrying to the end of the shower room when her feet slipped out from beneath her. She landed right on her behind with a loud bump and skidded directly beneath a powerful stream of water. "Aargh!" she yelped through a mouthful of water. A vision flashed in her mind of the school newspaper headlines: "Tragedy: Lacey Sinclair Drowns in Girls' Shower." "Aargh!" she gargled again, trying to scramble to her feet. Suddenly she felt a pair of hands grab her arms and start to pull her out from beneath the water. Once she was standing up, Lacey opened her eyes to see a tall, blond-haired girl, one she recognized as a junior cheerleader, smiling sympathetically at her.

"Are you all right?" she asked gently, handing Lacey a towel.

"I . . . I think so . . . ," Lacey's bottom lip quivered. "At least physically, I'm not hurt, but—" Her hand went up and felt her hair, which was plastered tightly against her scalp, dripping wet.

The blond girl smiled at Lacey once again. "Get dressed and meet me over by the mirror. We'll get you straightened out before second period."

Lacey nodded, grateful the girl hadn't laughed at her. She raced back to her gym locker and quickly pulled on her clothes, then wrapped a towel around her head like a turban. As she dressed, she bit her bottom lip to keep from crying, remembering all the extra work she had done earlier that morning to make her hair and makeup look perfect. Now, it was all ruined . . . what a disaster! She hurried over to the mirror, where the blond-haired girl was already waiting for her.

"I'm such a hopeless nerd," Lacey moaned, as she looked at her reflection in the mirror. She unwrapped the towel from around her head and moaned even louder. She looked like a drowned rat! Her hair was all matted down, and her mascara and eye shadow had been smeared all over her face—so much for waterproof makeup! Today had been the day she had hoped to get Kevin's attention. She would get his attention, all right. He'd take one look at her and either laugh hysterically, or run for the hills!

"You're not a hopeless nerd; the floor is slippery," the tall girl said, turning around to face her. "I'm sure we can repair the damage before the bell rings. By the way, my name is Glenna Wilks."

"I know," Lacey said shyly. "You're a cheerleader," she said, remembering Peg showing her Glenna's picture in last year's yearbook. "I'm Lacey Sinclair."

Glenna smiled fully, revealing a mouthful of perfectly beautiful, straight white teeth. In fact, Lacey had never personally known anyone quite as pretty as Glenna Wilks. Her hair was pale blond, cut in a bob, and her eyes were as blue as the sky on a cloudless summer day. Every single thing about her appearance was perfect. "Well, Lacey Sinclair, let's see what we can do." Glenna pulled a hairbrush from her purse and began brushing Lacey's hair. "While I'm working on your hair, get some makeup out of my purse. Use whatever you need."

For a few minutes the two were silent as they concentrated on making Lacey look presentable. "There!" Glenna announced just as the bell rang. "Your hair is still a little damp, but you look just fine. If I were you, I'd invest in a pair of rubber thongs for the shower. That way, there's less of a chance to slip," Glenna said as she quickly gathered up her things.

"Thanks for being so nice to me and helping me," Lacey said, collecting her books from the bench next to them.

"I'll tell you a little secret," Glenna whispered as the two girls left the locker room. "When I was a freshman, I fell underneath the shower, too!"

Lacey stared at Glenna in utter amazement. It seemed totally unbelievable that Glenna, a popular, beautiful cheerleader, could have something like that happen to her. Glenna saw Lacey's look of disbelief and laughed. *Even her laugh is musical and beautiful,* Lacey thought with a touch of envy.

"Lacey, believe me, everyone has bad luck sometimes." She stopped and turned to walk down another corridor. "I have to go left here," she explained. "To geometry. Ugh!"

"Thanks again for all your help," Lacey

said sincerely, awed by not only how pretty Glenna was, but also by how nice she seemed. And she had once fallen under the shower, too!

"No problem. It will be our little secret." Glenna smiled, then turned and walked up the corridor to her next class.

Someday I'd like to be just like her, Lacey thought as she hurried to her next class. It would be wonderful to be so popular and pretty and still be nice, too. Last year Lacey had noticed that many of the girls who were popular and pretty were so snobby that they wouldn't speak to anyone who wasn't in their own little group. Given the choice, Lacey would rather be known as being average and nice instead of beautiful and snobbish. Still, it would be great to be pretty, popular, *and* nice!

As Lacey sat in her third-period class, she began to doodle Kevin's name on a sheet of paper from her notebook. Her hand swirled across the paper, drawing in big, bold lettering, then in spidery, small print. She wrote his name in old English script, then in fat, bubblelike lettering. And the whole time she was writing his name in various ways, she was thinking about what would happen when she walked into psychology class.

She could see it perfectly. Kevin would

already be in his chair. He would look up at her, smile his wonderful smile, and then his eyes would brighten as he noticed the Van Halen T-shirt. "Hey, are you a Van Halen fan?"

"Sure," she would answer. "They're one of my favorite groups!"

"Mine, too!" He would smile as if seeing Lacey for the very first time. He would forget all about her being the same girl who had dumped her books in his lap and talked to him with mustard dripping off her chin. He would see her only as a nice-looking girl who liked Van Halen, a girl he would definitely like to get to know better!

"Van Halen is going to be in town for a concert sometime soon. Maybe you'd like to go with me?" he would ask, looking at her hopefully.

Lacey would smile at him, looking confident and self-assured. "I'd love to go to a concert with you," she would answer, and they would smile at each other again, and it would be the beginning of a wonderful romance!

It could happen, Lacey told herself. *Couldn't it?*

By the time she was hurrying to psychology class, Lacey was so excited she could hardly remember what room to go to. She had looked for Kevin all morning, and had even casually walked by his locker twice, but she hadn't had any luck. As she hurried down the stairs to the second floor, a sudden horrible thought struck her: What if he was absent today? What if that was the reason she hadn't seen him at all this morning? Then all her excitement would be for nothing. She'd have to wait another day before seeing him again, and two more weeks before wearing John's T-shirt again. Otherwise, everyone at school would think she didn't have any clothes! *He's just got to be there*, she thought to herself as she pushed open the classroom door. Lacey suppressed a tiny gasp of relief as she saw Kevin sitting at his desk. She lowered her books in her arms, so the logo on the T-shirt was plainly visible, then started slowly toward her seat behind him.

As she approached, he looked up and smiled at her. "Hey! Are you a Van Halen fan?" he asked.

"Sure," Lacey answered breathlessly, realizing the whole conversation was starting just like her fantasy. "They're one of my favorite groups." Lacey held her breath in anticipation. Now came the part where he would ask her to go to a concert with him. She sighed dreamily, then looked at Kevin.

"I used to like them a lot, but I don't think they're that good anymore," Kevin replied, turning his attention back to his psychology textbook.

"What happened?" Peg asked the moment class was over and the two were on their way to lunch.

"Nothing happened," Lacey said flatly. "He asked me if I liked Van Halen, I told him I did, and then he told me he *used* to like them, but he hates them now."

"And . . ." Peg prompted.

"And nothing. I sat down."

"Why didn't you keep talking to him, ask him what kind of music he does like?" Peg asked impatiently.

"Because I was mortified!" Lacey replied glumly. "Now he knows that I'm a nerd with no taste in music!"

The girls made their way through the lunch line, then took seats at one of the long tables. "Lacey, that's not true," Peg began. "First of all, all he knows is that you like Van Halen and he doesn't. Secondly, he must not think you're too much of a nerd. After all, he did start talking to you first. I think that's a good sign!" Peg said brightly.

"Really?" Lacey asked.

"Sure. If he thought you were a complete

nerd, he wouldn't have talked to you at all," Peg said, biting into her hamburger.

"Hi, Lacey!"

Lacey turned around to see Glenna Wilks waving to her from the next table.

"Hi, Glenna!" she called out. Then she turned back to Peg, who was staring at Lacey as if she had just seen a ghost.

"How do you know Glenna Wilks?" Peg said sharply once she had swallowed her food.

"We met this morning." Lacey started nibbling on a piece of lettuce from her chef's salad.

Peg looked at her curiously. "And I thought you needed help!" she scoffed. "You have the most popular girl in the junior class yelling hello to you across the lunchroom. You must be doing something right!"

Lacey giggled, thinking of how she had met Glenna. "I suppose you can say that, if falling under the shower in p.e. is doing something right!"

Peg's eyes widened. "You fell under the shower?"

Lacey nodded. "I got totally soaked. Glenna helped me look normal again."

"I thought your hair was different than it was this morning," Peg replied thoughtfully. She looked back over to where Glenna was sitting with a group of her friends. "She sure is pretty, isn't she?"

Lacey nodded, fishing a carrot out of her salad and placing it on the tray next to her bowl. "And the really neat thing about her is that she's so nice. She was the only girl in the whole locker room who offered to help me."

Peg turned her attention back to Lacey. "Okay, so what are you going to do about Kevin?" she asked.

Lacey shrugged her shoulders. "Nothing."

"Lacey, you can't give up so easily!" Peg protested.

"I'm not giving up easily," Lacey answered. "I tried to get him interested in me, but I failed. I am not going to make myself look like a fool in front of him *again*."

"Lacey, this is the second day of school. You've only seen Kevin a couple of times. You've got to give him a chance to work up his nerve and ask you out! It takes John days before he asks out a girl he's interested in. You know, guys get just as shy and nervous as girls do!"

Lacey chewed a bite of her salad, thinking about what Peg had just said. Was she right? Did guys get as nervous as girls did when it came to dating? It just didn't seem possible. Did Kevin find it as hard to talk to a girl as Lacey found it to talk to boys? "I suppose I could give it one more try," she said slowly.

"Good. And I'll think of another way you can get Kevin interested in you."

Lacey looked at her friend, doubtful. "I hope whatever you come up with works better than this stupid T-shirt idea."

"Don't worry, I'll think of something really terrific," Peg assured her.

Somehow, Lacey wasn't one bit assured!

Chapter 5

"Have you decided what committee you're going to work on for the Drama Club?" Peg asked, grabbing another handful of potato chips from the bowl that sat on the bed.

"I've been thinking about it since the meeting yesterday after school, but I'm still not sure what committee I want to be on." Lacey crunched a chip in her mouth. "Glenna told me she's going to audition for the first play."

"Yeah, I was thinking about trying out, too," Peg said, brushing off the pile of potato-chip crumbs that had collected beneath her. "Hey! I thought of something you can do to see Kevin. I found out he lives in Woodbury Estates. How about if you just casually walk by his house some evening?

He'd probably come out and talk to you if he saw you."

Lacey frowned at her friend. "Peg, Woodbury Estates is about five miles away from here. And what am I supposed to do when I get there? Just keep walking back and forth in front of his house until he comes out?"

"Maybe you're right. I guess that won't work," Peg agreed. "Well, then, why don't you have a party?" she suggested eagerly. "You could just invite Kevin, and then when he gets to your house, you could tell him that all the other people you invited had to cancel at the last minute."

"Get real!" Lacey looked at Peg in disgust.

"Lacey, you've got to do something." Peg jumped off the bed and began to pace back and forth across Lacey's bedroom floor. "The first week of school is almost over and everyone's starting to date already. You have to get Kevin interested in you before some other girl grabs him!"

"I know. But how?" Lacey said, feeling hopeless. She knew Peg was right. Kevin was such a good-looking guy, it wouldn't be long before some other girl noticed him.

"Have you thought about throwing your books at him again? You could just sort of pretend to trip. That would get him to notice you." Peg stopped pacing and looked at Lacey.

"No way!" Lacey shook her head fiercely. "I want him to look at me, not *laugh* at me, stupid."

"Oh, well, it was just a thought." Peg flopped back on the bed next to Lacey. "In the meantime, tomorrow night is the first varsity football game. Do you want to go?"

"Okay . . . sure," Lacey said after a moment's hesitation. She didn't know very much about football, but maybe if she went to the game, she could mention something about it to Kevin on Monday.

"Great! Mom said she would take us and pick us up afterward."

Lacey nodded. "I'll have to check with my mom, but I'm sure it will be okay." She sighed, still thinking about Kevin.

"Don't worry." Peg reached out and gave Lacey an impulsive hug. "We'll think of something, I'm sure of it!" Peg grinned confidently at her and grabbed another potato chip.

"Hey, Lacey! Wait up!"

Lacey turned to see Glenna Wilks hurrying down the hallway toward her, looking beautiful in a denim skirt and a brightly colored, geometric-patterned big shirt. "Since we're both going to p.e., there's no sense in walking there alone." Glenna smiled brightly and fell into step beside Lacey.

As the two girls walked toward the girls' locker room, Lacey felt a twinge of envy as she noticed how many guys smiled and spoke to Glenna. It seemed as if everyone knew her, and everyone liked her.

"So, have you decided what committee you want to work on for the Drama Club?" Glenna asked as they entered the locker room.

"Not yet," Lacey answered, setting her school books down on the long wooden bench, then groaning loudly as the books teetered and fell to the floor. "Oh, I'm such a klutz!" She stomped her foot with frustration, then bent down to pick up the books and papers that had scattered all over the floor.

"It's no big deal. Here, I'll help. Hey! What's this?" Glenna asked, looking at a piece of paper she had picked up off the floor.

Lacey felt a hot blush slowly climb up her neck as she realized Glenna was holding the piece of paper that had Kevin's name doodled all over it.

"Hmm, this Kevin must be someone special." Glenna smiled at Lacey, then turned her attention back to the piece of paper.

"It's really nothing, just some doo-dles. . . . ," Lacey mumbled, conscious that her face had turned bright red.

"No, I think this is really important," Glenna said slowly, looking at Lacey with admiration.

"What do you mean?" Lacey asked, a sinking feeling in the pit of her stomach. Had Glenna managed to figure out who Kevin was? After all, Glenna was a junior, and so was Kevin. Lacey would die if Glenna had figured out that Lacey liked Kevin Jamison. Not only that, but she spent her spare time doodling his name on blank sheets of paper.

"Did you write all these different scripts?" Glenna asked, her eyes still looking at the piece of paper.

"Well . . . yes . . ." Lacey admitted.

"Then I know what committee you've got to be on in the Drama Club. In fact, at the next meeting I'm going to recommend that you be put in charge of the posters-and-programs committee." She smiled at Lacey and handed her the sheet of paper. "You should have told someone that you're a pro at calligraphy. But I can tell that you're the modest type," Glenna said, taking out her gym suit.

Lacey smiled. She wasn't being modest—
she had no idea what the word "calligraphy"
meant!

Immediately following gym class, Lacey
hurried to the school library and grabbed a
dictionary, anxious to look up the word
calligraphy. She'd never heard it before.
"Calligraphy—the art of beautiful handwriting." She closed the dictionary and smiled
with a real sense of pride. For years,
whenever she had doodled, she had always
played around with creating new styles of
handwriting. She hadn't known that it took
a special talent or had a name.

For the first time in a long time, Lacey felt
really good about herself.

The feeling persisted as she walked into
psychology class later that morning. As
usual, Kevin had arrived before her and he
was already seated, his eyes scanning a
page in his psychology textbook.

"Hi, Kevin." Lacey surprised herself by
speaking as she walked by him to her seat.

Kevin looked up from his desk. "Hi,
Lacey."

"Don't you know you're supposed to read
the assignments before you get to class?"
she teased, gesturing to his open textbook.

"Yeah, but I forgot all about the reading
assignment until I walked into the class-

room." He smiled at her, that half-crooked, expanding smile that made her heart catch in her throat.

The teacher entered the classroom and Lacey quickly took her seat. It wasn't until she sat down that her hands began to shake as she realized she had actually started a conversation with Kevin.

For the remainder of the psychology class, Lacey sat and stared at Kevin's back, a glow of happiness lighting her face. She was fascinated by the way the fluorescent over-head lights made his dark, curly hair shine with red and gold highlights. Her fingers itched with the desire to reach out and touch one of his soft curls, and the very idea made her blush.

She was slightly disappointed when, as usual, class was dismissed and Kevin scooted off as if there were a fire under his chair.

"I've got it!" Peg cried, greeting Lacey after class. "I've discovered the perfect way for you to get to know Kevin better!"

"How?" Lacey said with a dubious grin.

"I found out that every Saturday Kevin and a bunch of his friends, including some girls, get together and play touch football in the park."

"What does that have to do with me?" Lacey asked.

"Tomorrow is Saturday. How about to-morrow morning you and I just casually take a walk in the park in the area where they all play football?" Peg looked at her eagerly.

"Oh, I don't know, Peg." Lacey hesitated. It was one thing to talk to Kevin in class, and it was quite another to actively plot to "accidentally" bump into him in the park.

"Come on, Lacey, it's a public park. We have every right in the world to take a walk there, and if we just happen to run into some kids from school . . . it will be a nice surprise!"

Lacey thought about it for a few more minutes. Then, remembering Kevin's friendly smile when she had spoken to him, she slowly nodded her head. "Okay. We'll take a walk in the park tomorrow morning. But if this little scheme doesn't work, it's the last time I'm going to try to get Kevin's attention!" Lacey warned Peg. She meant it!

"It's a deal!" Peg grinned widely, grabbing Lacey's arm and pulling her toward the lunchroom. "Now, let's eat. Coming up with these schemes always makes me hungry!"

Chapter 6

What a perfect night for a football game!
Lacey thought as she and Peg joined the
other Pep Club members in the middle
section of the home-team bleachers. The
sky was painted in colors of pinks and
oranges as the sun slowly sank in the
western sky, and the cool autumn breeze
made Lacey grateful that the club uniforms
included a pale blue, warm sweater.

Lacey looked around the bleachers at all
the people yelling and cheering. When she
took a deep breath, she smelled the scent of
freshly popped popcorn in the air. The huge
lights on the football field shined brightly
on the players as they lined up for the
starting kickoff.

Lacey knew very little about football, but

she found the excitement and the en-
thusiasm of the crowd contagious. Every
time the home-team crowd screamed, Lacey
stood up and yelled right along with them,
enjoying the feeling of being part of a crowd,
the feeling of belonging.

At half time, Lacey and Peg made their
way through the crowd and got in line at the
concession stand. "Hmm, the smell of that
popcorn has been teasing me all night long.
I've got to have a big box!" Lacey exclaimed,
her mouth watering at the mere thought.
She frowned for a moment. "Mom was too
busy getting ready for her date with Bill
even to think about fixing supper, so I'm
starving."

"All I want is a big soda and a candy bar,"
Peg said with an impish grin. "I'm having a
massive chocolate attack!"

"Haven't you heard that chocolate gives
you pimples?" Lacey asked with a grin.

"I think that's a horrible rumor," Peg said,
her impish grin growing wider. "I'm going
to start the rumor that doing homework
gives you pimples. Maybe my mom will hear
the rumor and demand that I never do a
minute of homework again!"

"Fat chance!" Lacey giggled, then sucked
in her breath when she spotted Kevin Jamison standing with a group of boys about

thirty feet away. Since he wasn't facing in her direction, she decided to observe him.

He looked incredibly handsome in a bulky navy blue sweater and a pair of jeans that hugged his long legs. As she stood watching him, he turned and his gaze caught hers. He smiled and raised a hand in greeting.

"Wave back, dummy!" Peg whispered.

Lacey smiled back and raised her hand slightly, then turned away as Kevin's attention was once again directed to his group of friends.

The rest of the football game flew by like a pleasant dream for Lacey. She didn't see Kevin again, but she kept replaying that moment in her mind when their gazes had met and he had smiled and waved. Was it possible he did like her just a little bit? After all, he could have pretended not to see her if he had wanted to. Nobody had forced him to wave at her!

Not only did Lacey consider the evening wonderful, but all of Oak Ridge High School went home happy after the football game. The Oak Ridge Raiders had trampled the other team, the final score being 21–0.

After the game, Peg and Lacey made their way through the crowd toward the parking

area, where Peg's mother would pick them
up.

"I didn't know football games were so
exciting," Lacey commented, her voice
slightly hoarse from all the yelling she had
done.

"It was great!" Peg agreed, sounding a
little like a bullfrog. "We'll never see my mom
in this crowd. We'd better just wait here for
some of the traffic to thin out." Her dark
eyes searched the parking lot for her mom's
bright red Thunderbird.

Lacey nodded, her gaze scanning the
people and cars in the parking lot. Football
was definitely a popular sport. It seemed as
though the whole town had turned out for
the game!

"Hey, Lacey!"

She turned around and felt her breath
catch in her throat. Kevin Jamison was
running toward her, a friendly smile on his
handsome face. "Hi, Kevin," she murmured
as he stopped in front of her.

"Great game, wasn't it?" His face was
flushed with excitement and he was standing so close to her that she could smell the
spicy scent of his cologne.

"Yes, it was very exciting," Lacey said,
wondering how on earth she was managing

to talk around the nervous lump in her throat.

He looked at her curiously. "You sound sort of funny."

She gestured to her throat and smiled. "I think I yelled too much," she explained.

He smiled again. "I know what you mean."

Lacey merely nodded, unsure what else to say.

At that moment a car full of guys pulled up before them. "Come on, Jamison!" somebody yelled, and the back door of the car swung open.

"Oh . . . I gotta go. Those are my friends." Kevin climbed into the car, and the car took off, but not before Lacey saw him turn around and wave to her out the back window.

When the car had turned out of sight, Lacey expelled a long, deep breath, for the first time realizing she must have been holding her breath the whole time.

Peg grabbed her by the shoulders and began jumping up and down. "Lacey, he likes you, he likes you, I just know he does!"

Lacey started jumping up and down, too. Her heart felt as if it were going to burst with excitement. Kevin had talked to her— he had walked right up and talked to her! She felt like dancing, she felt like singing, she felt happier than she had ever felt in her life!

At that moment Peg's mom pulled up, and Lacey and Peg tumbled into the backseat, giggling and elbowing each other in the ribs.

"Well, you guys seem like you had a good time tonight," Mrs. Simmons said, guiding the car slowly out of the parking lot.

"It was a fabulous night!" Peg exclaimed, hanging over the front seat like a little kid. "We won the game and Lacey has a boy-friend." She giggled as Lacey punched her lightly in the back.

"Buckle your seat belt, and who is Lacey's boyfriend?" Peg's mom asked teasingly.

"He isn't my boyfriend . . . yet. . . ." Lacey blushed as Peg buckled herself into the seat belt.

"He's not her boyfriend yet, but if Lacey has her way, he'll be her boyfriend by tomor-row night!" Peg giggled as Lacey elbowed her once again. "Anyway, the football game was really fun!"

"I'm glad you girls had a good time. That's what high school is for. Good times, football games, dances, and boyfriends." Peg's mom winked at Lacey in the rearview mirror. "Especially boyfriends!"

Lacey blushed again, but this time it

wasn't because she was embarrassed, but because she was happy. That same blush of happiness was still on her face when Peg's mom dropped her off in front of her house.

"I'll be over at ten o'clock in the morning and we can go for our walk in the park," Peg called after her pointedly, reminding Lacey that they had further plans to promote romance between her and Kevin. As if Lacey would forget!

Lacey paused on her front porch, watching until Peg's car was out of sight. Then she hugged herself and looked up at the starlit night sky. It had been a wonderful night, and even though it was getting late, she wasn't a bit sleepy. She was too excited by the thought that Kevin really might like her!

She burst through the front door, anxious to tell her mom what had happened. She practically flew into the living room, but the brilliant smile on her face faded slowly when she saw her mom and Bill sitting side by side on the sofa.

"Oh . . . hi," Lacey mumbled. She'd been anxious to tell her mom about Kevin, but she wasn't about to say anything with *him* sitting there.

"Hi, honey. How was the game?" her mom asked with a smile, making Lacey notice how pretty her mom looked. She had on more makeup than she usually wore, and she was wearing a pale blue ruffled blouse that Lacey had never seen before.

"It was okay. We won," Lacey answered, somehow irritated that her mom looked so happy sitting there next to Bill.

"Why don't you join us?" Bill suggested, moving over on the sofa to make room for her. "We're watching an old Jerry Lewis and Dean Martin movie. It's a classic comedy."

"No, thanks, I'm pretty tired. I think I'll just go right to bed," Lacey said coolly, turning to go to her room.

"Lacey . . ." Her mom's voice stopped her.

Lacey turned and faced her mother. Her mom looked at her as if she wanted to say something important, but after a long pause, she simply said, "Good night. Sleep well."

"Good night," Lacey answered. She went into her bedroom and closed the door.

As she undressed and got ready for bed, all of her happy feelings vanished as she thought about Bill and her mother. They sure were seeing a lot of each other lately, she thought as a deep scowl creased her face. Surely there was nothing serious between them. Surely her mom wasn't falling in love with Bill! The very thought made Lacey feel sick to her stomach.

She got into bed, her mind still whirling with thoughts of Bill. Lacey had gotten used to it being just her and her mom. They made a good team together, and they had made it on their own just fine since her father had died. They didn't need a man in the house, and Lacey certainly didn't want a stepfather!

She frowned at the sound of her mom and Bill's laughter coming through her bedroom door. For some reason the sound made Lacey feel very, very lonely. With a frustrated sigh, Lacey pulled her pillow over her head, trying to shut out the sound of laughter that echoed throughout the house.

Chapter 7

Lacey popped out of bed just after dawn and ran to her bedroom window. She had been convinced that it would rain and she and Peg would have to cancel their walk, but luck seemed to be smiling on her. The sky was a vivid blue and the sun was shining boldly over the horizon.

Lacey opened her bedroom window and breathed in deeply, enjoying the crisp autumn smell. Yes, it was going to be a beautiful day, even more beautiful because she was going to see Kevin.

She closed her window against the chill of the morning. For a moment her excitement vanished when she thought of her mother and Bill, and how happy they had looked together the night before. "No!" she said aloud, refusing to think of that particular problem. She wasn't going to let anything spoil this day for her!

Kevin . . . Kevin . . . Kevin . . . Her heart sang his name as she washed, then fixed her hair twice, not liking the way it had come out the first time. It took her even longer to decide what to wear. She couldn't really dress up because, after all, she and Peg were just going for a walk in the park. Besides, if things went well and they were invited to play touch football with Kevin and his friends, she didn't want to have to worry about ruining good clothes. She finally settled on a pair of jeans and a pale blue sweat shirt that brought out the vivid blue of her eyes.

Even after all that, Lacey was ready nearly an hour early. She wrote a note to her mother, who was still sleeping, telling where she was going. Then she went out onto the front porch and sat down to wait for Peg.

Never had an hour passed so slowly. She waved to Mr. Porter, the neighbor who came out in his robe to get the Saturday morning paper. She counted the cars that passed her house, trying to guess where each one was headed. Finally, she began to count the seconds and minutes, beginning with one-

one thousand, two-one thousand, three-one thousand. . . .

She had reached four hundred fifty-one thousand when she finally spotted Peg jogging down the sidewalk toward her house.

"All ready?" Peg asked brightly as she approached Lacey.

"I've been ready forever!" Lacey exclaimed, jumping up off her front porch and falling into step beside Peg. She noticed that Peg, too, had dressed in a pair of jeans and a sweat shirt.

It was about a fifteen-minute walk from Lacey's house to the park, and they took off at a brisk pace. They'd walked two blocks when Peg suddenly turned to Lacey with a wide grin. "I can't stand it any longer, I've got to tell you!"

"Tell me what?" Lacey asked absently, all her thoughts focused on what she was going to say and how she was going to act if she saw Kevin in the park.

"This morning Josh Alton called. He asked me out for next Saturday night!" Peg looked at Lacey expectantly.

As Peg's words sank in, Lacey stopped and turned to Peg. "Oh, Peg, that's great! Aren't you excited?" She hugged Peg happily.

"Sure, I'm excited," Peg said as they

started to walk again. "But now it's more important than ever that you and Kevin get together. I want *both* of us to be dating our dream guys!"

"What if they aren't playing today?" Lacey asked as they entered the Oak Ridge Town Park.

"Oh, I'm sure they're playing today. John left the house earlier and told me he was going to play football in the park as usual," Peg explained as she and Lacey skirted the playground area.

"Maybe this isn't such a good idea," Lacey said softly, feeling sort of sick to her stomach as she heard yells and laughter coming from the field just over the hill.

"Come on, Lacey, you've come this far. Besides, remember last night when Kevin came up to talk to you? I'm telling you, he likes you. All you have to do is give him the opportunity to ask you out, and this is perfect!" Peg grabbed Lacey's arm and pulled her along. Together the two of them crested the hill, and just below them, in the grassy field area, about twelve kids were playing football.

Lacey immediately spotted Kevin in the crowd. It was as if she had some sort of built-in radar tuned to him. He was wearing worn jeans and a blue sweat shirt and he seemed to be arguing with another guy, although neither of them sounded too angry.

"Come on, let's go a little bit closer," Peg urged, and they took a few more steps toward the field. It was at that moment that Kevin looked up and saw them.

"Hey, here's two more players!" He smiled at Lacey and Peg and gestured for them to come closer. "Lacey, you can be on my team, and your friend can be on John's team."

Lacey's legs felt like Jell-O as she walked over toward Kevin. He not only had invited her to play, but he wanted her on his team!

"Uh . . . I don't know very much about football . . ." she murmured.

Kevin smiled at her with his warm, wonderful smile. "It doesn't matter. It's just touch football, and we play for fun. Stick next to me and I'll tell you what to do."

"Hey! Are you two gonna stand there and grin at each other all day, or are we gonna play ball?" John yelled, causing a hot blush to steal over Lacey's face.

"We're gonna play ball!" Kevin laughed exuberantly.

At first, Lacey followed him around like a puppy dog, unsure what she was supposed to do when the ball came her way or when one of the other team members ran toward her. But Kevin was patient with her, explaining what was happening and different game plans. With his help, it didn't take her long to understand the basics of the game, and soon she was running and laughing with everyone else.

When they called a time-out, Lacey dropped down onto the grassy bank of the field, exhausted. Her heart did a series of flip-flops when Kevin sat down next to her.

"Are you having fun?" he asked, pushing his hair off his forehead, making it stick up in the front.

Lacey nodded, clasping her hands together in an effort to stifle an impulse to smooth down the front of his hair. "I'm not sure what I'm doing out there, but I'm having fun."

He grinned. "I don't think any of us knows what we're doing." He looked at her curiously, and for the first time Lacey noticed that his eyes weren't just a dark, chocolate brown, but had tiny little gold flecks in them. "So, what are you doing when you're not sitting in psychology class or playing Saturday morning football?"

Lacey shrugged. "Well, I just joined the Drama Club . . ."

"That's great! Are you an actress or something?"

She shook her head with a small blush. "No, I think I'm going to be on the committee that makes the posters and the programs. I'm sort of into calligraphy."

"Calligraphy . . . what's that?"

Lacey blushed again. "It's different kinds of handwriting."

Kevin's face lit up with recognition. "Oh, I know what you're talking about, like old handwriting, right?"

"Sort of like that," Lacey agreed.

"That's really neat. Maybe you'll show me some of it sometime," he said in a soft voice.

"Okay," Lacey said, and for a moment they just sat there and smiled at each other, unaware of the kids who were talking and laughing around them. "Uh . . . what do *you* do when you aren't sitting in psychology class or playing Saturday morning football?" Lacey finally asked, desperate to break the silence between them.

Kevin shrugged. "I do a lot of sports. I like movies, but most nights I end up baby-sitting my little brother."

"How old is your little brother?" Lacey asked curiously.

"He's six, and he's a real terror. He thinks he's the original Karate Kid. He's always coming up behind me and karate-chopping my back or kicking me in the shins."

Lacey giggled. "He sounds sort of cute."
She sighed. "I used to wish I had a little
brother or a sister. There's just my mom
and me," she explained.

Kevin laughed. "I sometimes wish I *didn't*
have a little brother. Most of the time Billy
follows me around like a little shadow."

"He must think a lot of you."

"Yeah, I guess maybe he does." Lacey
noticed that all the other kids were getting
up, ready for another round of football.
"Ready to play some more?" Kevin stood up
and held out his hand to Lacey.

Lacey's heart pounded frantically in her
chest as she reached up and placed her
hand in Kevin's. It felt so right to be holding
his hand, and once he had helped her up,
he didn't let go until they were out in the
center of the field and play had begun.

Across the field, Peg winked at Lacey,
letting her know that she thought things
were going well. For once, Lacey didn't need
Peg's vote of confidence. Kevin liked her; she
just knew he did. She had a feeling that
before the game was over, she'd have a date
with Kevin Jamison.

Lacey threw herself into the spirit of the
football game, ecstatic when she did something that made her team members—
especially Kevin—yell, "Nice try, Lacey!" Or:

"Way to go, Sinclair!" She knew her jeans were getting dirty and her light blue sweat shirt was now the color of brown mud, but she didn't care. Kevin liked her, and that was all that mattered.

They had been playing for about twenty minutes when Lacey found herself right in front of the goalposts with the football sailing in a big arc straight toward her. There was nobody around to stop her, nor was there anyone else to catch the football. Lacey, aware that her team members—especially Kevin—were depending on her, wiped her hands on her jeans and raised them up in the air. "I've got it!" she yelled as the ball flew closer and closer to her. "I've got it!" she screamed, jumping for the ball. The football never touched her hands. It smacked her square on the nose with a force that knocked her flat on her back.

She'd always heard of people seeing stars when they got hit on the head, and as she lay stunned on the ground with her eyes tightly closed, Lacey knew it was true about noses, too. She not only saw stars, she saw colorful fireworks and shooting rockets. It felt like the Fourth of July in her head!

She was vaguely conscious of the sound of running footsteps as all the other kids realized she was hurt.

"Lacey, are you all right?" Peg's voice rose above the exploding fireworks in Lacey's head.

She slowly opened her eyes and the sparkling lights in her head disappeared. Looking up, she saw everyone in a circle around her, staring at her with concerned eyes. She tried to smile reassuringly, but the effort made tears spring to her eyes as her nose began to throb painfully. It felt as if her nose was splattered all over her face!

"Lacey, are you sure you're all right?" Kevin asked, leaning down next to her, his forehead creased with worry.

"I'm fine." Lacey tried once again to smile and struggled up to a sitting position. The minute she sat up, she felt a warm trickle from her nose, and then a huge drop of blood fell onto the front of her sweat shirt. "Oh . . . !" she said as the first drop of blood was quickly followed by a second.

She looked up just in time to see Kevin quickly turn away from her with a disgusted look on his face. The pain that ripped through Lacey's heart was a thousand times worse than the pain in her nose. Lacey wanted to die!

Chapter 8

"Uh . . . I'd better go home," Lacey murmured, blinking back the tears that filled her eyes as she struggled to stand up.

Her nose was bleeding in earnest now, dripping through the hand she had cupped beneath it and staining the front of her sweat shirt.

"Here." John dug into his jeans pocket and pulled out a wrinkled, but clean handkerchief. Lacey took it from him gratefully and held it up beneath her nose. She looked at Kevin and saw he still had his head turned away, as if he couldn't stand the sight of her.

As tears spilled out of her eyes and down her cheeks, Lacey turned and ran for home.

"Hey, wait up!" Lacey heard Peg calling

after her, but she ran on without looking back. She was humiliated and in pain, and all she wanted to do was get to the safety and security of home and sob her eyes out.

As she ran, she kept the handkerchief firmly pressed against her nose, wondering if it was broken. What did doctors do for a broken nose? Did they put a splint or a cast on it? She moaned, imagining herself going to school with a great big plaster cast in the middle of her face. No, if they put a cast on her nose, she wouldn't go to school. She'd have her mom arrange for some sort of home-study program so she wouldn't have to go to school until her nose was back to normal.

She gasped as another thought struck her—maybe her nose would never be normal again! Maybe she would spend the rest of her life with a nose like the prizefighters on television had, all mushed and flat against her face. Maybe she could get a job and make enough money to get plastic surgery done on her poor, pitiful nose. Then, as she thought of Kevin, she wondered if plastic surgeons could fix broken hearts.

With all these horrible thoughts going around and around in her head, by the time she entered her front door, she was sobbing uncontrollably.

"Lacey?" Mrs. Sinclair came out of the kitchen, took one look at her daughter, and gasped in horror. "Honey, what on earth happened?" Without waiting for an answer, she guided Lacey into the kitchen and over to the kitchen sink. She took the bloody handkerchief away from Lacey's nose and gave her a handful of clean tissues. "Blow," she instructed Lacey.

Lacey did as she was told, blowing her nose into the tissues.

"Now, keep your head forward and pinch your nostrils together tightly."

The bleeding stopped almost immediately. Lacey's sobs had also stopped, and her mother guided her over to the kitchen table and sat her down in a chair. Lacey watched as her mom wet a towel with cool water and handed it to her. "Wash your face," she said gently.

Lacey ran the cool cloth over her face, grimacing with pain as she ran the towel lightly over her nose.

"Now, let me look at you." Mrs. Sinclair studied her daughter's nose with a professional nurse's eye. "Tell me what happened."

Lacey yelped as her mother ran her fingers lightly over her nose. "Ouch! Well, a bunch of us were playing football in the park and everything was going just fine, and then a pass was coming to me and I jumped up and held out my hands, and the ball hit me in the nose!" Lacey explained. She thought again of the disgusted look on Kevin's face. Everything had been going so wonderfully, but now it was all ruined!

Her mother pulled a chair up next to Lacey's and put her arm around her. Lacey laid her head against her mother's chest and cried, almost wishing she was a little kid again. When she had been about five years old, she'd believed her mom had magic kisses. Her mom had been able to kiss any boo-boo and make the pain go away. But she wasn't five anymore, she was fifteen, and she knew her mom's kisses couldn't take away the pain in her heart— and neither could any plastic surgeon.

"It's okay," her mom said soothingly, patting Lacey's back. "Your nose isn't broken, and although it's swelling a little bit, it should be fine for school on Monday."

Lacey nodded, but her mom's words didn't make her feel any better. She wanted to tell her mom that she wasn't just crying because her nose hurt, but she was crying because she had ruined things with Kevin.

However, that pain was too fresh to talk about at the moment.

"Why don't you get out of those dirty clothes, take a nice hot bath, and lie down for a while?" Mrs. Sinclair suggested. "I'm sure you'll feel better after a short nap."

Lacey nodded and slowly got up out of the chair. "Mom, is growing up always this hard?"

"What do you mean?" her mother asked, looking at her curiously.

Lacey frowned miserably. "Is it always one embarrassing thing after the other?"

"Yes, honey, I guess sometimes it is," she answered softly.

Lacey nodded, then went into the bathroom. She stared at her reflection in the mirror and once again felt her eyes fill with hot tears. No wonder Kevin hadn't been able to look at her. She looked totally gross!

Her eyes were all puffy and red from her crying and her mascara had run all over her face. Her hair looked as if she'd stuck her finger in an electrical outlet, it was all straggly, and grass and dead leaves were clinging to the blond strands. But her nose was the absolute worst. It was bright red and swollen to twice its normal size. Gone was her small, upturned little nose, and in its place was a clown's nose. All she needed was an orange wig and a clown costume and she could pass for Ronald McDonald!

She turned away from the mirror and dabbed the tears from her face with a tissue. She didn't blame Kevin for being disgusted with her. After turning on the water for her bath, Lacey stripped off her clothes, throwing the sweat shirt into the wastebasket. Her mom probably wouldn't be able to get the bloodstains out of the pale blue material, and even if she did, Lacey would never want to wear it again. It would only remind her of the worst day of her life!

She stayed in the warm bath for a long time. Her mom knocked on the door once to tell her Peg was on the phone, but Lacey didn't feel like talking, to anyone, not even Peg. She didn't want to see anyone. She only wanted to forget the whole humiliating experience. She wanted to forget all about Kevin Jamison and dating and everything. She was never going to have a date. She would never fall in love and get married. She'd end up an old maid like Mrs. Estes, the English teacher, and she'd dye her hair blue and have twenty cats.

She squeezed her eyelids closed and a tear slowly oozed out, falling off the tip of her Bozo nose and into the bathwater. She didn't want to be an old maid! She hated blue hair, and she was allergic to cats!

She climbed out of the bathwater and dried off, carefully avoiding her reflection in the mirror. Once in her bedroom, she pulled on her nightgown and crawled into bed. Her nose was throbbing and she felt absolutely miserable. Maybe her mother was right and she'd feel better after a little nap, but somehow she didn't think so.

Finally she did sleep, but as she did she dreamed about her nose. In her dream she was walking down the halls of the school and her nose was the size and color of a ripe tomato. Every time other students would walk by her, they'd reach out and squeeze her nose and it would make a horrible honking noise. Honk! Honk! Honk! Suddenly Kevin was standing right in front of her, and his chocolate-brown eyes were big and sad. "Gosh, Lacey, I'm really sorry," he began saying. "I was really beginning to like you a lot, but I can't date a girl who looks like Bozo the Clown." Then he reached up and squeezed her nose. Honk! Honk! Honk!

Lacey awoke with a start, surprised to find herself in her room and not in the hallways of Oak Ridge High School. She blinked, surprised that her room was semi-dark. She had slept away the whole afternoon.

She jumped out of bed and walked over to
the mirror, relieved to see that her nose
wasn't the size and color of a tomato. In
fact, must of the redness was gone, and
although it was still swollen and sore, her
nose didn't look half as bad as she had
expected. Still, no amount of time would
make the pain of her aching heart go away.
She would never, ever forget the look on
Kevin's face when her nose had begun to
bleed.

She turned away from the mirror. Her
stomach was rumbling hungrily. She
hadn't eaten any breakfast that morning
and she'd slept through lunch. A small
smile came to her lips. Her life was falling
apart, but her stomach still knew it was
dinner time.

"Hello, sleepyhead," Wanda Sinclair
greeted Lacey as she came out of her bedroom and into the living room. "How's the
nose?"

"Sore," Lacey admitted, flopping onto the
sofa next to her. "What's for supper? I'm
starving."

Her mother grinned, her blue eyes twinkling. "I thought maybe you needed a little
treat tonight, so I called up for a pizza. They
should be delivering it anytime."

"Hmm, that sounds good," Lacey said,

placing a hand on her stomach as it rumbled again.

"Now that you're a little calmer, would you like to tell me what happened?"

Lacey sighed. "Peg and I went to the park today because I knew there would be a guy there that I sort of like." Lacey felt her face turn pink, but she continued. "His name is Kevin, and I like him a lot. Anyway, everything was going really well, and he was talking to me and acting like he was really interested in me, and then the football hit me in the nose." Lacey's chest tightened painfully. "And . . . and I looked at Kevin and he turned away from me like he couldn't even stand to look at me." Lacey bit her bottom lip for a moment, her eyes on her hands, which were clasped tightly in her lap. "It was horrible. I feel so stupid."

"Honey, it was an accident. There's nothing for you to feel stupid about. My goodness, it could have happened to anyone!" Mrs. Sinclair pointed out.

Lacey shook her head. "Everyone always says that to me. 'Oh, Lacey, it could have happened to anyone.' But the point is, it always happens to *me!*" She frowned. "I'm the one with the bad luck! I'm the one who got the football in the face! And don't tell me it's just a stage I'm going through and someday I'll outgrow it!" She glared at her mom, daring her to say the same old tired words of comfort.

Wanda Sinclair looked at her unhappy daughter and sighed. "Lacey, you asked me earlier if growing up was always so hard, and I told you it was, and it is! I think being a teenager is the hardest thing a person goes through in her life. Some days you're so happy you feel like your head's in the clouds, and other days you're so down in the pits you don't think you'll ever be able to climb out. But you've got to remember that you're not alone. The girl sitting next to you in your English class, the boy who's the school jock, the cheerleaders at the football games, and the boy who sits next to you in math—they all have the same feelings that you have. They all worry about getting pimples and going out on dates and becoming popular. It's just a part of the process of growing up." She was interrupted by the ringing of the doorbell. "And that's probably our pizza." She gave Lacey's hands a quick, supportive squeeze, then got up to answer the door.

Lacey wanted to believe what her mother had just told her, but it all seemed pretty hard to swallow. She couldn't imagine somebody like Glenna Wilks worrying about getting dates. She couldn't imagine any of the other cheerleaders crying themselves to sleep because they had done something stupid and were afraid everyone would laugh at them. Lacey knew her mom was only trying to help. But Lacey knew there was nobody else in the whole world who felt as badly as she did that night.

It was almost midnight when Lacey's mother finally shut off the television and sat back down on the sofa. She faced Lacey, who was sitting on the floor. "Lacey, we need to have a serious talk," she began.

"What about?" Lacey asked, nibbling on some leftover crust from their pizza.

"About Bill."

Lacey put down the piece of pizza, suddenly losing her appetite. "What about him?" she asked faintly.

"How do you feel about him?" Mrs. Sinclair asked, looking at Lacey searchingly.

Lacey shrugged. "I don't know. Do we have to talk about him tonight?" she asked.

"Yes, I think we do." Her mom paused, then continued softly. "Lacey, you know I loved your father with all my heart."

Lacey nodded, feeling more and more afraid as she wondered where the conversation was leading.

"When your dad died, I think a part of me died, too." Her mom was silent for a moment, and Lacey knew she was remembering the wonderful man to whom she'd been married. Lacey's heart ached as she remembered the many nights right after her dad's death when she and her mom had held each other and cried. Her mom looked at her for a long moment, then continued. "Lacey, your dad has been gone for a long time now. I've grown to care a great deal about Bill, and last night he proposed to me."

"Proposed!" Lacey's eyes widened in disbelief. "You didn't accept, did you?" The fear that had been a vague ache in her chest suddenly exploded.

"No, but I think I'm going to," her mom answered. "Lacey, honey, I know this is sort of a shock, but—"

"A shock!" Lacey interrupted. "It's a total catastrophe, that's what it is!" She jumped to her feet and ran for her bedroom, ignoring her mother calling her.

She threw herself on her bed, fighting back the tears that burned in her eyes. How could her mother do this to her? How could she even think of getting married again? How could she marry Bill? Once they were married, nothing would ever be the same again! There would be no more nights with just the two of them eating pizza and laughing at old movies. There would be no more cozy girl talks over cups of hot cocoa. "I'll be a third wheel," Lacey whispered aloud. Her mother wouldn't have any time for her anymore with Bill around. It would be horrible!

Her mom knocked softly on her bedroom door. "Lacey, we need to talk."

"There's nothing to talk about," Lacey replied, hiding her head in her pillow as her mom opened her bedroom door.

"Yes, there is." Mrs. Sinclair walked into the room and sat down on one side of Lacey's bed. "Lacey, I'm sorry if my news upsets you." She stroked Lacey's hair lovingly. "But Bill is an extremely nice man, and I think he'll make me—and you—very happy."

Fat chance! Lacey thought, but she didn't say anything.

"Give him a chance, Lacey. The three of us could be a happy family." She paused a moment longer, then stood up. "Think about what I've said and we can talk more tomorrow." With these final words, she left Lacey's bedroom, closing the door behind her.

When she was gone, Lacey rolled over on her back and stared up at the ceiling. She felt empty inside. Kevin would never, ever like her, and her mom was going to have a new husband. Had anyone in the whole world ever had such rotten luck?

Chapter 9

"I'll get it!" Lacey yelled when the phone rang early the next morning. "Hello?"

"Uh . . . Lacey? This is Kevin—Kevin Jamison."

"Oh, hi, Kevin." Lacey's heart began to beat wildly at the sound of his deep voice.

"How's your nose?" he asked.

"Fine." Lacey blushed, not wanting to be reminded of the horrible football incident.

"Well, I was wondering if maybe you'd like to go to the movies with me next Friday night."

"Why?" Lacey blurted before she thought. "I mean . . . the way you acted yesterday when I got hurt . . . I didn't expect you would want to go out with me. . . ." She let her voice trail off in embarrassment.

There was a long silence on the other end of the line, and for a second Lacey thought he'd hung up on her.

"Kevin?"

"Yeah, well . . . about yesterday . . . promise you won't tell anyone what I'm about to tell you?" He paused, waiting for her answer.

"Sure," Lacey answered without hesitation.

"I faint at the sight of blood." He laughed nervously. "Stupid, huh? It's something I just can't help. I see blood and I get dizzy, and then before I know it, I faint!"

Lacey wanted to scream, she was so relieved. He hadn't been disgusted by her; he'd been disgusted by the blood!

"Lacey? I guess you don't want to go out with me."

"No! I do! I'd like to go to the movies with you!" she exclaimed. "I mean, if you still want to go," she added nervously.

"Sure, I still want to go!"

For a moment there was an uncomfortable silence between them.

"Well . . . uh . . . I guess I'd better go," Lacey finally said, afraid she would say something stupid and he would change his mind.

"Okay. I'll see you tomorrow at school," Kevin said. " 'Bye, Lacey."

" 'Bye, Kevin." Lacey slowly hung up the phone, then whooped with joy. She had a date, her very first date! And it was with the boy of her dreams! She had to call Peg, and tell her, right away. Life was looking up!

"Isn't this exciting? We both have dates for the weekend!" Peg greeted Lacey the next morning on the school bus.

Lacey flopped down in the seat next to Peg, excitement making her eyes sparkle brighter than usual. "I still can't believe it," she whispered.

"Well, believe it! Next Friday night you'll be out with Kevin, and I have a feeling it will be the beginning of a wonderful relationship!" Peg squealed and gave Lacey a quick hug. "It looks like all your bad luck is finally behind you!"

Lacey's smile faded slowly and her eyes darkened. "Not quite," she replied softly.

"What are you talking about?" Peg looked at her curiously.

"My mom is getting married."

Peg's brown eyes widened in surprise. "You're kidding me!"

Lacey shook her head with a sigh. "I wish I *were*. She told me last night that Bill had proposed. Then this morning she told me they're planning the wedding in about six months. She's even going to put our house up for sale!" Lacey said bitterly. Her mom had dropped that bombshell over breakfast.

"You're going to move?" Peg squeaked in panic.

"Don't worry. We're just going to move into Bill's house. He lives on Sycamore Street, so it's only a few blocks from where we live now. But that's not the point." Lacey scowled, thinking of the changes that were taking place in her life, changes she didn't want! "I think this is the worst thing that's ever happened to me."

Peg grinned at her impishly. "Worse than getting hit in the nose with a football?"

Peg's good-natured teasing made Lacey laugh. "Let's just say it's a tie." She giggled as they got off the school bus. As soon as she and Peg had parted ways, Lacey hurried to her locker, surprised to find Kevin waiting for her. When she saw him she slowed down, wanting to have a moment or two just to look at him before she had to concentrate on talking to him. He looked so handsome. He was wearing a pair of stonewashed denims and a brown-and-gold plaid shirt.

"Hi," he said, his smile widening as she got closer.

"Hi, yourself," Lacey answered, wishing she could control the blush that always warmed her cheeks whenever she talked to him.

"How's your nose?" he asked as she opened her locker and placed her books inside.

"A little bit sore," she admitted, slamming her locker shut and turning to face him.

"Which way is your first class?"

"The gym."

"Come on, I'll walk you to class." He touched her lightly on the elbow and guided her down the hallway.

Every day Lacey had seen couples going to classes, girls and guys walking together, talking and laughing as if they were the only two people in the hallways. Now, she was finally one of those couples. She looked up shyly at Kevin, wondering if he thought it was as exciting as she did. Probably not. Guys didn't get excited about the same sort of things as girls.

"Lacey, I want to apologize again for the way I acted when you got hurt on Saturday," he said as they walked slowly down the hall together.

"It was no big deal." Lacey shrugged,

finding it easy to forgive him. "I just didn't know you got sick at the sight of blood."

"Nobody knows it," Kevin said quietly. "I mean, my parents know about it, but they're the only ones. Last summer my little brother fell off his bicycle and skinned up his knees pretty badly. Mom sat him down at the kitchen table and told me to watch him so she could get a wet washcloth from the bathroom." He laughed, a short, embarrassed burst of laughter. "My brother was crying his eyes out and the blood was pouring from his knees, and I looked at all that blood . . . and zap . . . the next thing I knew I was flat on my back on the kitchen floor, and mom was putting a wet towel on my head and another on my brother's knees." The red on his cheeks deepened. "Dumb, huh!"

"I just hope you aren't planning on becoming a doctor," Lacey commented with a sympathetic smile.

"No way!" He laughed and they came to a stop in front of the girls' locker room. "If you wouldn't mind, I'd rather nobody knew about how blood makes me sick." He looked down at the floor, then anxiously back at her. "The other guys would really give me a bad time if they knew."

Lacey saw the worry on his face. He was

afraid his friends would make fun of him, laugh at him. She could understand that fear very well! "I promise I won't say anything to anyone," she said sincerely, happy that she and Kevin had a secret to share.

"Thanks." He grinned at her, then frowned as the warning bell rang. "I gotta go or I'm going to be late. I'll see you in psychology class!" He took off at a fast-paced jog down the hall. Lacey watched until he was out of sight. Then, releasing a happy sigh, she went into the locker room. She jumped as somebody poked her in the back. Turning around, she saw Glenna Wilks smiling at her.

"I'll bet I can guess by the look on your face that the Kevin Jamison who just walked you to class is the same Kevin whose name was written all over that sheet of paper."

Lacey nodded. "Do you know Kevin?"

"Just a little. He seems like a real nice guy." Glenna grinned at her. "And speaking of that sheet of paper, I still intend to nominate you for head of the posters-and-programs committee at this week's Drama Club meeting."

Lacey wanted to protest. She wanted to say that she wasn't capable of that sort of responsibility, that she couldn't handle

being the chairman of a committee, that
her bad luck would make her do something
wrong. But she felt too happy and excited
about Kevin to allow herself any self-doubts.
"I'd like to be chairman," she answered,
then looked curiously at Glenna. "How come
you're so nice to me?" she asked suddenly.

"Oh, I don't know. I think you're a pretty
nice kid, and you sort of remind me of when
I was a freshman," Glenna admitted.

Lacey opened her mouth to ask her how
she, bad-luck Lacey, could possibly remind
the beautiful, popular Glenna of herself, but
just then the bell rang and, with a quick
wave, Glenna ran toward her locker. Lacey
quickly changed into her gym clothes,
knowing she was going to be late for class,
but somehow not caring. After all, Kevin
Jamison had walked her to class!

Later that morning, Kevin was waiting for
her outside the psychology classroom, and
once again Lacey felt a thrill as he smiled
his wonderful smile just for her.

"Hello, again," she said as she approached
him. "Have you read your psychology assignment, or do you need to jump into your
seat and read it now?"

"No." Kevin laughed, his brown eyes

sparkling with the golden flecks she had noticed for the first time on Saturday. "I read what I was supposed to last night, which means the teacher won't ask me any questions. He only asks me questions when I'm not prepared and haven't read the assignment."

Lacey giggled. "You mean stuff like that happens to you, too?"

"Sure, I think stuff like that happens to everyone." Kevin gestured toward the classroom as the warning bell rang. "We'd better go in." They walked into the classroom and took their seats and Kevin instantly turned around to finish talking to her. "I'm not sure what movie we'll see on Friday night. I'll let you know later in the week."

"Okay," Lacey answered warmly.

"And I won't be able to walk you to lunch after psychology. I help some of the coaches out by organizing the sports equipment during lunch," he said, explaining why he always took off after class as if he were racing to a fire.

"What do you do about lunch?" Lacey asked curiously. She could never go through a day of school without eating.

"Mom sends me a sandwich." He held up a brown-paper bag on top of his school books.

He turned around as the final bell rang and the teacher entered the classroom.

"I nominate Lacey Sinclair for chairman of the posters-and-programs committee," Glenna Wilks announced to the members of the Drama Club on Wednesday afternoon.

Lacey grinned at Glenna, then closed her eyes as the vote was taken by a show of hands. As Lacey's name was called by the club's president, Peg squealed happily and Lacey opened her eyes. "Lacey Sinclair is voted chairperson. Lacey, will you stand up?" The president of the club smiled at her as she rose with a deep red blush. "Okay, let's break into our committees." The president banged his gavel on the table, announcing the official end of the general meeting.

"I'll meet you out front after the meetings," Peg said as she hurried toward the area where the costume committee was meeting. Peg had auditioned for a part in the first play, but she hadn't gotten one, and had chosen to work on the costumes instead.

Lacey made her way up the stairs to the stage, where her committee would meet. The first thing she did was write down the names and telephone numbers of the four kids on her committee. When she had their names and numbers all written down in a notebook, she looked hesitantly at them. "I guess the best place to start is if everyone tells me what they'd like to do." She thought for a moment. "Somebody will have to do the artwork for the posters, and somebody the lettering. Uh . . . somebody will have to distribute the posters in school and around town." She frowned a moment, trying to think of all the jobs her committee would have to do.

"Somebody will have to write up the programs. I could do that," offered Monica Foster, the editor of the school newspaper.

"And my dad has a friend who owns a print shop. I could check out prices and stuff for the printing of the programs," added Scott Baxter.

"Great! I can do the lettering for the posters, but I can't do artwork." Lacey looked hopefully at the two kids left.

"Don't look at me for artwork," Mike Hanlon protested. "My mom once mistook a tree I'd drawn for a stickman break-dancing."

"I could do the artwork," Julia Mason said.

"Then all that leaves is distributing the posters," Lacey said.

Mike Hanlon grinned as all four committee members turned and looked at him. "I guess that's me."

"Great. I guess that's all we have to do today." Lacey closed her notebook. "Why don't we all bring in samples of our work next week and Scott can bring us some price quotes?"

"And I'll bring in my beautiful face for all of you to gaze upon," Mike said, making them all giggle.

"I'll see you all next week," Lacey said, proud that the first meeting had gone so well.

Lacey found Peg waiting for her, and together they left the theater and went out into the parking lot to wait for Peg's mother.

"How was your meeting?" Lacey asked.

Peg frowned. "Costume committee is going to be pretty stinky for this first play." Her eyes lit up. "But I heard that the musical this year is going to be *Oklahoma*. It should be a blast to find all the old-time clothes and cowboy stuff for that!" She turned and looked at Lacey with an impish grin. "How was your committee meeting, Miss Chairperson?"

"Fine." Lacey laughed with pleasure. "I'm really excited about doing all the posters for the play, even if it is going to be a lot of work."

"I'll bet I know something else you're excited about." Peg grinned slyly at Lacey.

"What?" Lacey asked, pretending she didn't know what Peg was referring to.

"Day after tomorrow, you're going to have your first date with none other than Kevin Jamison!"

Lacey looked at Peg and shrugged nonchalantly. "What makes you think I'm excited about a little thing like that?" Then she crossed her eyes and effected a look of complete panic, making her teeth chatter with nervousness.

As Peg's mom pulled up to the curb before them, both girls dissolved into a fit of giggles.

Chapter 10

Lacey frowned at her reflection in the dressing-room mirror. The brown-striped sweater and camel-colored skirt made her look like an old secretary or a schoolteacher going to work.

"No, I don't think that will do at all." Lacey's mother voiced the same opinion.

Lacey got out of the outfit and grabbed the next one, an acid-washed denim skirt and a blouse with tiny blue hearts, contrasting with the darker blue background.

Lacey had told her mom about her date that morning, and her mom had insisted they go shopping after school. Lacey knew this was her mother's way of trying to bridge the uneasiness that had lingered

between them ever since she had announced her marriage plans.

They'd been shopping for the past two
hours, and Lacey still hadn't found the
perfect outfit. What did a girl wear on a date
to the movies with the boy of her dreams,
anyway?

Most of the dresses she tried on were too
dressy for a date at the movies. Yet, the
jeans and sweaters she saw all seemed a
little too casual. What she needed was a
store that tagged their clothes with signs
like: "These clothes are perfect for a date to
a school dance." Or: "These clothes are great
for a date at the movies." Something like
that would certainly make dressing for a
date much easier, especially for girls who'd
never been on a date.

She sighed and shimmied into the denim
skirt, then pulled on the blouse and looked
at her reflection. A small smile began to play
on her mouth. This was it! This was the
outfit for her to wear on her date with
Kevin. She turned and looked expectantly at
her mom.

"Perfect!" her mother announced, making
Lacey's smile widen. "Take it off, hand it to
me, and I'll go pay for it while you change
back into your own clothes."

Lacey handed the new outfit to her

mother, then began to put her clothes back on. As she dressed, her mind whirled with excitement. In less than twenty-four hours she would be on her date with Kevin. He'd told her at school that he would pick her up at seven o'clock. She shivered with nervousness, then finished dressing and went out to meet her mother.

"Honey, this shopping trip took longer than I expected, and I'm supposed to meet Bill at his office. I'll drop you off at home and then I'll go on to meet Bill. Will you be able to find something for supper?" Mrs. Sinclair asked once they were back in the car and headed for home.

"Don't worry about me," Lacey said stiffly. She had consciously avoided the subject of Bill while they had been shopping. In fact, they hadn't discussed him at all since her mother had told Lacey she was putting their house up for sale and they would eventually be moving into Bill's larger home. Now Lacey felt resentment building inside her once again. She'd have to go home and eat alone because her mother was meeting Bill. And it would be a lot worse when they were married. Lacey's mom would never have time for her!

It was only a few minutes later that she waved good-bye to her mother, then shifted her packages into one arm as she ambled up the front walk and fished in the bottom of her purse for her house keys. She'd almost reached the house when Peg jumped out of the bushes. "Boo!" Peg screamed, giggling as Lacey jumped, frightened.

"That's not funny, Peggy Marie Simmons!" Lacey huffed, placing a hand over her heart. "You could have given me a heart attack!"

"Fifteen-year-old girls don't have heart attacks!" Peg rolled her eyes. "Where have you been? I decided to surprise you with a visit, but when I got here you weren't home. I was just about to leave when I saw your car pull up."

"Mom took me shopping," Lacey explained, unlocking the front door and stepping inside the house. "I got a new outfit for my date with Kevin."

"What'd you buy? Let me see!" Peg grabbed for the bags in Lacey's arms.

"If you ruin my new outfit with your grubby hands, I'll kill you!" Lacey laughed, wrestling the shopping bags away from her friend. She opened one and withdrew the skirt.

"Oh, Lacey, I've been wanting one of these!" Peg grinned at Lacey like a faithful puppy dog. "Have I ever told you that you're my best friend in the whole wide world?"

Lacey giggled. "Yes, you can borrow it," she said. "But not until after tomorrow night."

Peg squealed as Lacey withdrew her new blouse. "Oh, I love it!"

"You can borrow it, too, but only—"

"After tomorrow night." Peg finished the sentence for her and flopped down on the sofa.

"Are you getting excited about your date with Josh?" Lacey asked, carefully folding the clothes and putting them back in the bags.

"Sure. We're going to see the new Sylvester Stallone movie. It's supposed to be all blood and guts." Peg made a face. "What are you and Kevin going to do?"

"We're going to a movie, too, but I'm not sure which one." Lacey sat down on the sofa next to Peg.

"You'll probably see the same movie. All the guys at school have been talking about it."

Lacey shook her head, knowing Kevin would never go see a blood-and-guts movie. "I don't think so," she said. "Anyway, you're welcome to borrow my new outfit for your date on Saturday night."

"Thanks." Peg's gaze flitted around the living room, landing on several sheets of poster board that were leaning against the wall. "What's that?" she asked curiously.

"Last night I started working up samples of posters for the Drama Club," Lacey explained. She got up and grabbed the three sheets of poster board. "I lettered one in Black German lettering, one in Roman lettering, and a third in a combination of the two," she explained, showing each one to Peg.

"Wow! Lacey, these are really great!" Peg stared at her friend, admiration in her eyes.

"Thanks." Lacey felt very proud of her new found talent. "I'm going to take these three samples into next week's Drama Club meeting. Then the kids on my committee will vote on which style we'll use."

"Just think, a week or two ago you were sure that Lacey's Law was going to ruin your life. It looks like your bad luck is behind you now."

"Sort of," Lacey replied, thinking of her mother's plans to remarry. "At least things are going well at school, even if things here at home are stinky."

"Stinky? What do you mean?" Peg looked curiously at her.

"I just can't believe my mom is going to

get married again! I can't believe Bill is going to be my stepfather." Lacey sat back down on the sofa. "I don't see why we have to sell this house and move in with him. Isn't this house good enough for him?"

"Have you seen Bill's house? Maybe you'll like it even better than this one," Peg suggested, looking sympathetically at Lacey. "Maybe it won't be so bad,"

Lacey stared at Peg in disbelief, but said nothing. Of course Peg wouldn't understand. After all, she had her real mother and father at home. She wasn't going to have to move out of her favorite house. She wasn't going to have to get used to a stepfather!

"At least you've got a date with Kevin to look forward to," Peg said brightly.

This thought caused a smile to return to Lacey's face. Yes, even if her home life was falling apart, she had a date with Kevin!

At five minutes before seven, Lacey sat on the edge of her bed, waiting for her first real date to arrive. Her makeup had gone on smoothly and, for once, her hair had come out perfectly the first time. Her outfit looked nice, and she had put pink nail polish on her fingernails just for the occasion.

She liked Kevin so much, and this date was so important. She wanted things to be perfect, but she couldn't help thinking, *If anything can go wrong, it will.* She shoved this thought from her mind, concentrating on what Peg was always trying to drum into her head. Optimism. The date was going to be wonderful, Kevin was going to be wonderful, and she was going to be wonderful! Nothing was going to go wrong. Her bad luck was behind her for good. The fact that Kevin Jamison had asked her out proved it!

"Honey, it's almost seven." Wanda Sinclair popped her head in the doorway of Lacey's bedroom and smiled brightly. "You look very nice."

"Thanks." Lacey looked nervously at her mother, noticing how pretty she looked in a new peach-colored dress. "So do you."

"Bill and I are going out." Her mother laughed. "Isn't this fun? Both of us Sinclair women having dates for the evening!"

Lacey smiled stiffly. She didn't think it was fun, she thought it was gross! Her mom was much too old to be so happy about a date!

The doorbell rang and Lacey jumped.

"You wait here and I'll let him in," Mrs. Sinclair said smoothly.

Lacey got off the bed and went to the door, listening as her mother opened the front door and greeted Kevin.

"Have a seat," her mom was saying. "Lacey will be right out."

"Thanks, Mrs. Sinclair." Kevin's voice sounded deep and strong, sending a chill of excitement dancing up and down Lacey's spine. The palms of her hands were suddenly damp and her heart was beating wildly. This was it . . . the night she had dreamed about for so long, the night she had hoped for . . . her date with the hunk of her dreams. "Please let everything be perfect," she said softly.

"Hi, Kevin," she said shyly as he jumped up out of his chair. Oh, he looked so handsome! A gold sweater hugged his broad shoulders and brought out the gold flecks in his brown eyes. His dark hair was combed neatly, and as he looked at her his warm smile lit up his face. It seemed so strange to see him right here in her living room instead of in the crowded, noisy hallways of school!

"Hi, Lacey. You look great." He blushed, and then Lacey blushed.

"I'm sure you kids are anxious to be off." Lacey's mother came to the rescue, breaking the awkward moment by opening the front door for them. "Have a good time. And Lacey remember your midnight curfew."

Both Kevin and Lacey nodded. Then

Kevin smiled at Lacey. "Ready?" She merely nodded, and together they left the house and went outside.

"I've got my mom's car," Kevin explained, gesturing to the blue sedan parked at the curb. "I don't have my own car yet," he said in apology.

"That's okay," Lacey said hurriedly. She would have gladly ridden on the back of a horse with him! As he opened the passenger's door for her, she slid in, watching as he walked around to the driver's side.

"I thought we'd see the new Chevy Chase movie," he said as he got into the car and started the engine. "It's supposed to be really funny."

"That sounds good. I like Chevy Chase," Lacey replied. She'd never been in a car alone with a boy before, and it was weird, so different from being in the car with her mother.

"Uh . . . it's a nice night," Kevin said as he drove down the street toward the center of town.

"Yes, it is . . ." Lacey wished she could think of something witty or wonderful to say, something that would make him laugh, or make him think she was the most interesting girl he'd ever met. "Uh . . . I really like the fall," she added, finally desperate to make conversation.

"Yeah, me, too." Kevin gave her a quick, small smile, then directed his attention to pulling into a parking place in the parking lot of the Oak Ridge Cinema IV.

Once inside the movie theater, he led her down the aisle, then gestured to the two seats next on the aisle. "All right with you?"

Lacey nodded and sat down, her heart beating with excitement as he sat down next to her, his knees brushing against hers, his shoulders pressing against her own.

"How's your little brother, the Karate Kid?" She asked, turning slightly in her seat to look at him.

Kevin grinned. "He's not the Karate Kid anymore. Now he's decided he's G.I. Joe. So now I'm getting ambushed instead of karate-chopped."

Lacey giggled. "He sounds like he keeps your life interesting."

Kevin's smile deepened. "He definitely does that! You'll have to meet him sometime. He thinks most girls are pretty creepy, but I think he'd like you." He smiled warmly at her.

Moments later the theater lights dimmed and the movie credits began to roll. As soon as the movie had started, Kevin's hand reached over and covered hers, and Lacey wished the movie would last forever.

This was what she'd dreamed of for so long, sitting in a darkened theater with a boy she liked, holding hands. Lacey tried to concentrate on the movie, but she couldn't think of anything but Kevin. Every time he moved and his broad shoulder brushed her, her heart seemed to stop in her chest. He laughed and Lacey laughed, loving the sound of his easy, natural laugh. They even found all the same things funny!

He likes me, she thought happily, as he smiled at her and squeezed her hand, then looked back at the movie. *He likes me and everything is going perfectly. This is the happiest night of my whole life,* she thought, stealing a shy look at him from the corner of her eye.

At that moment, Chevy Chase took a hilarious pratfall and the audience roared with laughter. Lacey frowned, recognizing a very familiar laugh coming from someplace behind her. She slowly turned a little bit in her seat and gasped. There, sitting two rows behind her were her mother and Bill!

Chapter 11

Lacey quickly turned back around and stared blankly at the movie screen. What were her mom and Bill doing there? How embarrassing! How humiliating! *Let me die!* Lacey thought miserably. Of all the movie theaters in the world, why had they picked this one? She peeked at Kevin from the corner of her eye. What would he think? That her mom and Bill didn't trust her and had to check up on her? Oh, this would ruin everything! Lacey bit her bottom lip to keep the tears of humiliation from falling from her eyes. Her mom marrying Bill, moving out of her house—those things were bad enough, but this . . . this was disastrous!

"Wasn't the movie great?" Kevin enthused

as they walked through the lobby of the theater. "How about we head for The Pizza Place? Movies always make me hungry."

"That sounds good," Lacey answered faintly, walking fast, trying to make it out of the theater before they ran into her mom and Bill.

"Hey!" Kevin laughed and took hold of her arm. "What's your hurry? Slow down!"

Lacey blushed. "Sorry," she mumbled. "I guess I'm just hungry."

"Lacey, isn't that your mom over there?"

Lacey cringed as she saw her mom and Bill walking toward them. *Just let me die right now*, Lacey thought miserably.

"Hi, you two! If we'd known you were coming here, we could have all come together," Mrs. Sinclair said, smiling. Lacey's eyes widened with horror as she noticed her mother and Bill holding hands. It was so embarrassing that two adults were acting like lovesick teenagers!

"Lacey, aren't you going to introduce me?" Bill asked, smiling at Kevin.

"Kevin Jamison, this is Bill Weatherby, my mom's . . . uh . . . friend . . ." Lacey stumbled over the words.

Lacey's mom laughed. "He's a little more than my friend," her mom chided her, then smiled happily at Kevin. "Bill and I are going

to be married next February." Her mom
leaned against Bill and smiled tenderly at
him. "We're planning on a Valentine's Day
wedding."

"That's great! Congratulations." Kevin
and Bill shook hands, and Lacey wanted to
sink into the floor and disappear. A tinge of
anger rose in her chest. This was supposed
to be her night, her very first date with her
dream guy, and there she stood in the
middle of a theater lobby, hearing her date
congratulating her mother on her upcom-
ing wedding! It wasn't fair! It just wasn't
fair!

"We thought we'd have a small ceremony,
but it could be done really nicely with the
Valentine's Day theme," her mom continued
excitedly. Lacey watched her mom with
disgust. How could a grown woman act
so . . . ridiculous? Next thing Lacey knew,
her mom would be talking about their
honeymoon plans!

"We were just going to get some seafood.
Would you two like to join us?" Bill asked
with a friendly smile.

"No, thanks," Lacey said quickly. "Kevin
really has his heart set on pizza." She
looked desperately at Kevin. "Shouldn't we
be going?"

"Uh . . . sure." Kevin looked curiously at

her, then smiled at her mom and Bill.
"Maybe another time, okay?" he suggested
as Lacey turned to leave. He practically had
to run to catch up with her as she pushed
open the exit door.

When they were back in his car, Kevin
turned to her with a look of confusion. "Did
I miss something back there?"

"I'm sorry," Lacey apologized, feeling miserable. "I shouldn't have hurried off like
that, but I didn't want to go with them to
eat seafood."

Kevin grinned at her. "It's no big deal. I'd
rather not spend our first date with your
mother, either." He started the engine. "Besides, I really do have my heart set on pizza.
It's great about your mom and Bill getting
married," he commented, pulling out of the
theater parking lot.

"We'll see how great it is when Bill is my
stepfather," Lacey said bitterly.

"I gather you don't like Bill?" Kevin asked
curiously. Then he added, "I thought he
seemed like a nice guy."

"Oh, sure, he seems nice enough now, but
everything will be horrible when he and
Mom are actually married! I just can't believe my mom is getting married again. It's
like she's forgetting all about my real dad."

"Are your mom and dad divorced?" Kevin asked, coming to stop at a red light.

"No," Lacey said painfully. "My dad died."

"Oh, wow, I'm really sorry." Kevin turned to her, his brown eyes soft with sympathy.

"He died five years ago in a plane crash," she explained. They both jumped as a car honked behind them, signaling Kevin that the red light had changed to green. He started driving again.

"Gosh, Lacey, I'm really sorry about your dad." He was silent for a moment, then continued. "But five years is a long time. It's a long time for your mom to be alone."

"She wasn't alone! She had me!" Lacey replied, her voice trembling with emotion. "And we were doing just fine, the two of us. I don't need another father. I don't want another father. I don't want Bill in our lives!" she finished vehemently.

"Lacey, take it easy!" Kevin reached out and touched her arm softly. "I didn't mean to get you all worked up!"

"I am worked up—this whole thing works me up!"

"Well, isn't what your mom wants important, too?" He asked. "I mean, if something ever happened to my dad, I'd want my mom to be happy, to remarry eventually if she wanted to. I wouldn't want her to spend the rest of her life all alone."

Lacey stared incredulously at him. This wasn't the way she'd imagined her first date. Kevin should be on *her* side, not her mother's. He should understand how she felt! "You just don't understand," she said finally. "Nobody understands."

"I guess I don't." Kevin shrugged his shoulders. "I just know that I would want whatever made my mom happy. I wouldn't want to be selfish."

"Are you saying I'm being selfish?" Lacey asked tightly, angry with Kevin. She realized things were getting out of control, but she couldn't prevent it. The whole evening had been ruined.

"No, I'm not saying you're selfish," Kevin protested. "I guess I'm sort of a romantic. I think it's nice that your mom has found somebody to love again." He shrugged again. "She sure looked happy with Bill."

"Kevin, please take me home now. I'm really not hungry after all," she said, too miserable to eat.

"Are you sure?" Kevin asked, his voice as soft as hers had been.

Lacey nodded, biting her bottom lip. The night had been ruined, and there was no reason to prolong it. Lacey's first date had turned into a nightmare. The whole date had been ruined by her mom and Bill. She hated Bill! Now things were ruined between her and Kevin. She knew she had disappointed Kevin by getting so angry, but he had disappointed her, too. He was supposed to be her dream guy; he was supposed to understand how she felt about her mom's marriage. He should have understood how embarrassing the whole night had been for her.

"Lacey." Kevin turned to her as he parked the car in front of her house. "I'm sorry if I made you mad. I just think you're overreacting to your mom's marriage. I'm sure it's hard to accept another man in your mom's life, but if he makes your mom happy, isn't that all that's important?"

"What about what makes *me* happy?" Lacey blurted out.

He sighed and ran a hand through his thick brown hair. "I guess it's really none of my business."

"You're right—it's really none of your business!" Lacey stumbled out of the car and ran to her front door, unable to hold back her tears any longer. She heard Kevin calling her name, but she ignored him, quickly unlocking the front door and slipping inside.

Chapter 12

Lacey leaned against the front door, sobbing in despair. Everything was ruined! Pulling herself away from the front door and peering out the window, another sob caught in her throat. Kevin's car was gone. She went into her bedroom and threw herself on her bed, glad her mom wasn't home yet. She didn't want to talk to anyone.

More tears oozed out from beneath her eyelashes. Kevin would probably never ask her out again, and even if he did, she wouldn't go. She couldn't date a boy who thought she was selfish.

With a heavy heart, she changed into her pajamas and crawled beneath the covers on her bed. It seemed as if all her bad luck had built up and exploded in one night. Bad luck . . . she was definitely having more than her share. She rolled over on her back, thinking about her mom and Bill, then thinking about what Kevin had said to her. Were her feelings about her mom's remarriage all wrong? Should she be happy for her mom?

"No," she whispered aloud, as fresh tears trickled down her cheeks. She was going to have to share her mom with somebody else. She was going to have to move to a new house.

She wiped the tears off her face with the back of her hand and pulled the sheets up around her neck as she heard Bill and her mother come into the house.

"Lacey?" her mom whispered, sticking her head into the darkened bedroom. Lacey held her breath, keeping her eyes closed and pretending to be asleep. After a moment, her mom left the room.

As Lacey lay there, listening to the sounds of her mom and Bill talking and laughing in the living room, more tears fell from her eyes. Any other time her mom would have realized that something was wrong. After all, she was home and in bed way before her midnight curfew. But now, her mom was too anxious to be out in the living room with Bill to worry about her. Lacey squeezed her eyelids tightly closed, wishing she could fall asleep and forget all about her mom, Bill, Kevin—everything!

"So?" Peg asked when Lacey answered the phone the next morning.

"So what?" Lacey asked, dreading the next question.

"So, tell me all about your date last night—and don't leave anything out!" Peg demanded impatiently.

"There isn't much to tell," Lacey hedged.

"What do you mean, there isn't much to tell?" Peg said indignantly. "You finally get a date with your dream guy, and now you're saying there isn't much to tell? Give me a break!"

"We went to the movies. Then he brought me home." Lacey said.

Peg was silent for a moment. "What movie did you see?"

"The new Chevy Chase movie," Lacey replied.

"I've heard that's really funny," Peg said brightly.

"Yeah, it was a lot of laughs," Lacey said sarcastically.

Peg picked up on the tone of Lacey's voice. "You didn't like it?"

"The movie was fine," Lacey answered

impatiently, wanting to get off the phone before she started to cry.

"Lacey, what's the matter? You sound sort of upset. Are you and your mom fighting?"

Lacey laughed humorlessly. "Mom is too busy with Bill and their big wedding plans to fight with me."

"Well, something's wrong," Peg observed. "Lacey, we've been best friends for five years, and I know when you're upset. Did something happen between you and Kevin last night?"

"I don't want to get into it right now," Lacey said, hearing her mother approach from the living room.

"Did he kiss you good-night?" Peg asked in a lowered voice.

"No," Lacey answered flatly.

"Lacey, you make me so mad sometimes!" Peg protested heatedly. "I know something's wrong! Are you sure you and Kevin didn't have a fight or something?"

"Peg, I said I didn't want to go into it right now. I have to go." Without waiting for an answer, Lacey quickly hung up the phone. She turned as her mother entered the kitchen.

"Good morning," her mom said as she started making a pot of coffee.

"Morning," Lacey mumbled, unable to

forget how humiliated she'd been the night before.

"Lacey, we need to talk." Her mom wasn't smiling, and Lacey knew the conversation was going to be a serious one. She looked expectantly at her mom.

"Lacey, I've tried to be patient about the way you have been ignoring my plans to get married. I kept telling myself that all you needed was a little time to adjust. But you aren't adjusting." Her mom sighed and ran a hand through her curly hair. "You haven't even given Bill a chance. You're hardly civil to him when he's here. I want you to start trying a little harder."

"What do you want me to do? Throw my arms around him and call him Daddy?" Lacey exploded.

"Of course not! Nobody is expecting you to accept Bill as your father. You had a father, a man I loved very much, but he's gone, and he's been gone for a long time." Her mom sat down next to her at the table and took her hand. "I'm not asking you to let Bill take your father's place in your heart. All I'm asking is that you give Bill a chance to become a part of our lives. He's really a very nice man." She patted Lacey's hand. "Now, Bill is coming over for dinner this evening, and I want you to be here."

Lacey nodded, knowing this wasn't a request, but an order.

"Lacey, I want you to be as happy as I am."

"Yeah, sure." Lacey smiled bitterly.

"Lacey, would you pass the spaghetti to Bill?" Wanda Sinclair asked with a pleasant smile.

Lacey nodded and passed the bowl of spaghetti and homemade sauce to the man sitting next to her.

"I've been thinking," Bill began, serving himself a large helping of the spaghetti. "Wouldn't it be fun if this summer the three of us took a vacation at a lake and did some fishing?" He looked at Lacey's mom and grinned. "You said you'd like to learn how to fish."

"That sounds wonderful." Wanda Sinclair beamed.

"I hate fishing," Lacey blurted.

"Lacey! How do you know you hate fishing? You've never even been fishing before," her mom pointed out.

Lacey shrugged, a blush on her face. "I just know I'd hate it," she mumbled.

"That's all right. We'll go someplace else for our vacation," Bill replied easily. "Lacey, where would you like to go?" He smiled at her softly.

"I'd really like to go to my room." Lacey looked at her mom. "May I be excused?"

Her mom looked at her with disappointment and started to say something, then just nodded.

Lacey fled from the kitchen and into her bedroom. She knew she had disappointed her mom, but she didn't care! Seeing her mom and Bill smiling at each other and looking at each other tenderly had only made Lacey realize how alone she was. Kevin was gone, and her mom would soon have a new husband. Lacey sniffled back a fresh wave of tears and went over to her bedroom window. She stared out at the sky. She and her mother had been planning a vacation to Disneyland, but now they would end up at some stupid lake with fishing poles. Her mom wanted her to be as happy as she was, but how could Lacey possibly be happy when Bill was ruining her life?

At least my posters turned out well, Lacey thought as she carried them toward the high-school theater for the Drama Club meeting on Monday afternoon. She hurried up on the stage, where the members of her committee were already seated at the table waiting for her.

The meeting went well, and she should

have felt enormously satisfied by how smoothly she was handling the chairmanship of the committee. But she didn't.

After the meeting she met Peg as usual out in front of school. "Lacey, we need to talk," Peg said immediately.

"Talk about what?" Lacey asked hesitantly, knowing exactly what Peg meant.

"We need to talk about Kevin." Peg placed her hands on her hips and glared defiantly at Lacey.

Lacey flushed angrily. "There's nothing to talk about," she said firmly, carefully keeping her eyes averted from Peg's.

Peg snorted in disbelief. "Don't give me that! Why are you being so mean to Kevin? He told me you've been avoiding him all day. I thought you really liked him!"

Lacey shrugged, still not looking at Peg. "I made a mistake. We don't have anything in common. That's all."

"You mean because he thinks you're being hard on your mom's boyfriend?" Peg looked at her knowingly. "He told me all about your conversation with him. He knows we're best friends, and he wanted to know how he could make up with you."

"There's nothing to make up. We're just not right for each other." Lacey's heart ached at these words. "Besides, he should have been on my side, not my mother's!"

"Even if you're wrong?" Peg asked.

Lacey stared at her best friend. "You, too? Why is everyone against me?" she asked, stomping her foot angrily. "It's easy for you to think Bill is great; he isn't going to be your stepfather. You won't have to cope with him changing the rules, and planning vacations, and making things miserable!"

"How do you know Bill is going to do all that?" Peg asked her curiously.

"Because it's just my luck!" Lacey laughed. "With my kind of luck, he'll probably give me an eight o'clock curfew!"

Peg stared incredulously at Lacey. "You know, last year when you came up with that Lacey's Law stuff, I thought it was pretty funny. But it isn't funny anymore."

"You're telling me!" Lacey sneered sarcastically.

"I'm serious. Lacey's Law isn't the problem. *You're* the problem!" Peg's tone softened a bit. "Lacey, you're my very best friend in the whole wide world, but lately there are times when I can hardly stand to be around you. You're always looking for bad things to happen to you. You're always anticipating bad luck and you never give yourself any credit for the good things you do. You don't need any enemies; you're your own worst enemy. You look for problems before they even happen! You make your own bad luck!"

"If I'm such a horrible person, how can you stand to be my friend?" Lacey's voice quivered with hurt and anger. "Besides, you aren't always the most fun person in the world to be around, with your stupid lists!" Lacey replied, wanting to hurt Peg as much as her best friend had hurt her.

Peg's face turned pale. "I didn't know you thought my lists were stupid," she said, the sparkle gone from her dark brown eyes.

"And I didn't know you found it so hard to be around me," Lacey returned, the hurt and anger swirling around inside her.

"Well, maybe it would be best if we didn't spend so much time together," Peg said coldly.

"Maybe you're right. Maybe we shouldn't spend *any* time together," Lacey replied. "I think I'll just walk home." With her back rigidly straight and biting her bottom lip so hard it hurt, Lacey juggled her stack of books and her posters in her arms and started walking away.

Lacey wished Peg would call after her and she would run back and they would apologize and take back all the hateful things they had said to each other. But Peg didn't call after her, and she didn't stop walking. Instead, she walked until the school was out of sight and only then did she allow her tears to fall.

What was Lacey going to do now? What was she going to do without Peg? She and Peg had been best friends since fourth grade, when they'd discovered they both hated a snobbish, blond-haired classmate named Erica. Erica had moved away, but the friendship between her and Peg had lasted. *Peg and I are like sisters,* Lacey thought, kicking an autumn red leaf that fell to the sidewalk at her feet. *What am I going to do without her?*

Then she remembered what Peg had said to her. How could Peg be so mean, telling her she made her own bad luck! "Who needs her, anyway?" Lacey muttered, shifting her books and her posters in her arms. Who did Peg think she was, talking to her like that? Lacey thought angrily, sniffling back her tears. If Peg couldn't understand her bad luck, then she really wasn't a very good friend at all!

"Oh, no," Lacey moaned, dropping one of her posters to the ground. She bent over to pick it up, but lost her balance and promptly planted a dirty sneaker footprint right on top of the beautiful lettering. It was the last straw. With a strangled cry of anger, she picked up the poster and ripped it into tiny shreds.

Chapter 13

The next morning when Lacey climbed on the bus, the first person she saw was Peg, sitting with another girl. As Lacey made her way to an empty seat, Peg turned to the girl next to her and said something, and the two of them laughed. Lacey sat down in the empty bus seat and stared out the bus window. *Who cares?* she said to herself. *Who cares if Peg sits with somebody else? I didn't want to sit next to her anyway*, she thought defiantly.

Who cares? she thought again as she entered her psychology classroom later that day and both Kevin and Peg ignored her; refusing to look in her direction. *I don't need either one of them*, Lacey said to herself, opening her textbook and blankly staring at a page.

Yet, in spite of herself, Lacey found herself studying the back of Kevin's head during class, wishing things could have been different. Then, her gaze drifted over to Peg, and she felt a painful heaviness in her heart.

When the class was over, both Peg and Kevin hurried off in separate directions, and Lacey walked to the cafeteria. It was scary to feel so alone, she thought as she got a tray and went through the lunch line. For the past five years, she and Peg had shared everything: records, clothes, dreams, secrets. . . . Without Peg, Lacey felt as if half her heart was missing, and the other half had been broken in two by Kevin. She paid for her lunch, then walked out into the noisy, crowded lunchroom. Almost immediately she spotted Peg, sitting with a group of girls across the room. Their gazes met and for a moment Lacey could have sworn she saw a dark shadow pass across Peg's face, but then Peg turned to talk to the girl next to her.

Lacey slid into a seat at the end of a long table. *Nobody sits alone in the lunchroom,* she thought miserably, taking a small bite of her hamburger. Even the nerds at Oak

Ridge found one another and sat together at lunchtime. All around her she could hear the sounds of talking and laughter, and it made her feel even more lonely. *Just my luck*, she thought, taking another bite of the cold hamburger. *It's just my stupid bad luck that's the cause of everything!* She envisioned the days to come, more solitary lunches, no friends, no Kevin . . . it was more than enough to make Lacey lose her appetite. She shoved her tray away and looked up at the big clock on the wall. Fifteen more minutes and lunchtime would be over. At the moment, fifteen minutes seemed as long as an eternity!

"Hello, I'm home!" Lacey called as she came into the house late on Wednesday afternoon.

"Hello," her mother said as Lacey walked into the living room.

Lacey stopped short at the sight of Bill and her mother sitting on the floor by the coffee table, a huge pizza box in front of them.

"You're just in time! Bill brought over a huge, extra-special pizza with everything." Wanda Sinclair grinned.

"Uh . . . I think I'll just go to my room," Lacey mumbled. They probably wouldn't want her hanging around with them, any-way.

"Lacey, don't run off to your room," Bill protested. "It's covered with mushrooms, just the way you like it." He smiled shyly at her. "I'd really like for you to join us."

Lacey hesitated. Part of her didn't want to hang out with Bill and her mom, but the past two days had been the loneliest days of her life, and at the moment, even their company was preferable to another lonely night in her room. "Okay," she agreed, setting her posters next to the television, and sitting down on the floor.

"How come you're so late getting home this afternoon?" Her mother asked, opening up the pizza box and handing out paper plates and napkins.

"I told you, I had a Drama Club meeting," Lacey replied. *But of course you don't remember my telling you, because you're too busy with Bill*, she added in her mind.

"That's right, I'd forgotten," her mom admitted. "How did the kids like your posters?"

"What posters?" Bill asked curiously, smiling at Lacey as her mother placed a large slice of pizza on his plate.

"I'm chairperson of the posters-and-programs committee for the Drama Club.

We're working on posters for the first play. I'm doing all the lettering," Lacey explained, her mouth watering as she looked at the hot pizza.

"That sounds like an important job," Bill commented. He scowled as he took a bite of the pizza and cheese dripped down his chin. "Oops!" He grabbed his napkin and wiped his chin, then smiled sheepishly at Lacey and her mom. "I knew that was going to happen. In front of the two women I want to impress most, I manage to string cheese down my face."

Lacey and her mom looked at each other, and suddenly Lacey began to giggle. As Lacey's giggles grew louder, her mother began to giggle, too, and soon Bill joined them and all three were laughing loudly.

"Somehow I've got the feeling that you two are laughing *at* me, not *with* me," Bill said when they had all stopped laughing.

"Who? Us?" Her mom looked incredulously at Lacey, her eyes twinkling in mock innocence.

As Bill grinned at them both, Lacey noticed that he had nice blue eyes beneath the glasses he wore.

"So, show me these posters you've done," Bill said after they had all eaten their fill of the pizza.

"They really aren't any big deal," Lacey said embarrassed.

"Nonsense! I think they're terrific," her mother objected.

Lacey shrugged and got up to get the posters. She unrolled each one and held it up for Bill's inspection.

"You did all that lettering yourself?" Bill asked.

Lacey nodded.

"Lacey, these are good. Really good." He smiled at her and once again she noticed that despite his thinning hair and eyeglasses, he really was a nice-looking man. "You know," Bill began thoughtfully as Lacey set the posters back against the wall, "having my own insurance agency, I'm always distributing flyers and pamphlets to attract new clients. I could really use your talent when I get ready for the next batch." He looked at her expectantly, then added, "Of course, I'd pay you for your work. And I know talent doesn't come cheap!"

Lacey felt good for the first time in days. Bill was offering her a job, and she would be paid real money for her talent! How exciting!

As Lacey got ready for bed that night, she felt more confused than before. She'd enjoyed the night, and that was what bothered her. She got into her pajamas, then crawled into bed and stared up at the darkened ceiling.

Have I been wrong about Bill? she wondered. *It's true he makes Mom happy.* Lacey thought about the way her mother's eyes sparkled, and the laughter that never seemed to be very far from her when Bill was around. Yes, he made her mom happy.

Flopping over on her stomach, Lacey hugged her pillow to her chest. *Is it possible that some of the things Peg said were true? Do I focus too much on the negatives, causing my own bad luck?* Maybe Kevin had been right all along. Maybe she *was* being selfish in worrying about Bill's being her stepfather. Bill really wasn't a bad guy.

Lacey sat up in bed, suddenly realizing what a fool she'd been. She'd let her worries about Bill ruin things with Kevin. Now she was risking losing her best friend because of her stubbornness and stupidity. *It's not too late*, a small voice said inside her head. *Call Peg and apologize.* Lacey turned and looked at the clock radio on her nightstand. She sighed in disappointment and lay back down. It was after ten o'clock, too late to call Peg.

"There's always tomorrow," she whispered

aloud to the darkness of her bedroom. Tomorrow she would make up with Peg, and she would see if she could mend things with Kevin. The mere thought was enough to make her fall asleep with a smile on her face.

Lacey got off the school bus and waited by the front door of the school for Peg, anxious to put things right with her friend. She'd wanted to talk to her the minute she'd gotten on the bus, but Peg had been sitting in the back, and Lacey had had to take an empty seat in the front. She watched eagerly as the bus emptied, and Peg finally jumped down the steps. But Peg swept right past her without even giving a glance in her direction. By the time Lacey opened her mouth to say something, Peg was gone.

Okay, Lacey consoled herself. *I'll try again later*. She could understand why Peg had gone by her so fast. After all, Peg hadn't known she wanted to apologize.

Lacey hurried to her locker, deciding she would make a point to talk to Kevin and Peg *before* psychology class. She felt better just thinking about talking to them. It would be great to have her dream guy and her best friend beside her once again. She stored her books in her locker, and began walking down the corridor toward the gym.

Then she saw them. They were walking in the opposite direction, and for a moment Lacey simply stood and stared at their backs. Kevin had his arm around Peg's shoulders and their heads were close together. They looked so right, as if they belonged with each other.

Lacey watched them until they disappeared around a corner. When had that happened? How had that happened? Peg had mentioned that Kevin had talked to her, that he knew they were best friends. Had he talked to Peg about Lacey, then gotten interested in Peg? Had Peg run by her so quickly this morning because she was feeling guilty about falling in love with Lacey's favorite guy in the world? Lacey turned and stumbled in the direction of the girls' locker room. It was just Lacey's luck! She had waited too long to make up with them, and now they had fallen in love with each other!

Chapter 14

Lacey locked herself into one of the bathroom stalls just as the tears began to run down her face. Luckily for her, no one else seemed to be in the locker room. All she needed now was for somebody to come in and find her crying like a little baby. Lacey's sobs came in huge gulps that echoed in the tiny bathroom stall.

It was all too much to bear. Her mom had Bill, Peg had Kevin, and she was all alone. She knew her eyes were going to be all swollen and red, and her tears were probably making a mess of her makeup, but she couldn't stop crying.

She couldn't really blame Kevin for falling for Peg, with her cheerful attitude and sparkling brown eyes. Peg would never be selfish; she was too good a person for that.

"Hello? Are you all right in there?" There was a soft knock on the stall door and Lacey recognized Glenna's voice.

"It's all right . . . I'm all right." Lacey tried to sniff back her tears.

"Lacey, is that you?" Glenna knocked on the door again. "Lacey, what's the matter?"

"Really, I'm all right," Lacey called through the door, not wanting Glenna to see her crying.

"You don't sound all right. Open the door. Please," Glenna said softly.

Lacey slowly opened the stall door and stepped out.

"Do you want to talk about it?" Glenna asked gently, giving Lacey a handful of tissues and leading her over to a bench where they could sit down.

"There's nothing to talk about." Lacey's voice quivered and she immediately began to cry again. "Oh, Glenna, everything is just so messed up!"

"What's messed up?" Glenna asked, handing Lacey another tissue.

Lacey gulped deeply and wiped at her tears with the tissues. "It all started out when my mom told me she was going to get remarried. You see, Bill is this guy she's been seeing for a while."

"And you aren't happy about the marriage?" Glenna asked.

Lacey shook her head, then paused thoughtfully. "I'm not sure how I feel about it now. I hated the idea of a stepfather until yesterday, and I hate the idea that we're going to have to move into his house, and everything's all messed up with my boyfriend and my best friend, Peg."

Tears filled her eyes again. "I just feel so alone. My mom has Bill, and now Kevin likes Peg, and I don't have anyone at all."

Glenna smiled at her. "I know exactly how you feel."

Lacey looked at Glenna, surprised. "You do?"

"Lacey, I have a stepfather, and I remember feeling all the things you are right now. I wanted my mom to be happy, but I wasn't sure how things were going to be with a new man in our life—in our house!"

She laughed as Lacey stared at her in shock. It was so hard to believe that beautiful, perfect Glenna had a stepfather!

"Lacey, lots of people have stepparents nowadays. And I can still remember how scared I was when it happened."

"I'm not scared," Lacey protested. "I . . . I just don't like Bill."

Glenna smiled patiently at her. "I didn't like my stepdad, either, or so I thought. I couldn't understand what on earth my mom saw in him. After a while, I began to realize that I didn't hate him, I was just scared." Glenna put an arm around Lacey's shoulder. "I was scared that he was going to take my mom away from me somehow. I was scared that he and my mom wouldn't want me around anymore." Glenna laughed. "Pretty crazy, huh?"

Lacey stared at Glenna and shook her head in wonder. Scared . . . was that what she had been feeling? She could honestly say that deep down in her heart, she really didn't hate Bill. In fact, she'd liked him the other night when the three of them had shared the pizza. Instead, she'd been afraid, afraid that Bill and her mom wouldn't want her around anymore.

"I feel sort of stupid," she confessed to Glenna in a soft voice. "I guess you're right. A lot of what I've been feeling has been fear. Logically, I know my mom loves me more than anything on this earth, but I was afraid that Bill would change all that."

Glenna nodded. "Sometimes our emotions don't listen to logic."

"Thanks, Glenna." Lacey smiled at her warmly. "At least you've helped me understand things better. I'll give Bill a chance to become a part of my life." Her smile slowly faded as she thought of Kevin and Peg. "I just wish I hadn't waited until it was too late to fix things between Kevin and me."

"Are you sure it's really too late?" Glenna asked softly.

Lacey pictured Kevin and Peg walking down the hall together, their heads so close, his arm around her. She nodded miserably as a wave of despair swept over her. "Yes, I'm sure."

"Hello," Lacey called when she finally walked into the house after school, grateful that the day was finally over.

"In here," her mother's voice called out.

Lacey entered the kitchen, where her mother was busy cleaning out the oven. "Hi, sweetie." Her mom wiggled a hand covered with a glove and smelly white foam in Lacey's direction.

"Looks like you're busy," Lacey commented, sitting down at the kitchen table.

"I have a realtor coming over Saturday morning. It's time to put the house on the market. How was school today?" her mother asked, her head disappearing back into the oven as she scrubbed the blackened inside.

"Okay," Lacey answered, trying to forget the whole miserable day. It seemed as if every place she had gone all day, Kevin and Peg had been there together, looking happy. So . . . uh . . . what kind of plans are left to be made for this big wedding of yours?" She almost giggled aloud as her mother raised her head too fast, bumping it on the top of the stove's interior.

"Oh . . . well . . . we've already decided on the colors of red and white, but I still need to pick out my dress and decide on the flowers," Mrs. Sinclair stuttered, obviously shocked by her daughter's sudden interest.

"Well, I was just sort of wondering if maybe you needed a maid of honor, because I'm available," Lacey announced.

Tears of happiness sprang to her mother's eyes. "Oh, Lacey, do you really mean it?" Lacey nodded, giggling as her mom rushed across the kitchen and embraced her in a tight bear hug. "Honey, I'd be thrilled if you'd be my maid of honor." She squeezed Lacey even more tightly.

"Mom, if you really want me to be in your wedding, then you'd better let me go right now," Lacey said, "because the fumes from that stinky foam cleaner in your hair are about to kill me!"

Her mom's hands flew up to her head,

where they touched the white sticky foam clinging to her short, curly hair. She looked at Lacey, and together they burst out laughing.

"Lacey, I'm leaving for work now." Her mom poked her head into Lacey's bedroom, where Lacey was stretched out on the bed doing homework. "I won't be home until after midnight. Make sure you don't stay up too late. It's a school night."

"Okay, Mom," Lacey replied absently, concentrating on the algebra problem in front of her.

"Bill may be bringing some things over later. We're planning a garage sale in a week or so. We've accumulated a lot of unnecessary junk over the years." She looked pointedly around Lacey's cluttered room. "It wouldn't hurt you to gather up a box or two of stuff to get rid of."

"Okay," Lacey repeated, looking up from her books in time to see her mother leaving the room. "Have a good night at work!" she yelled after her mom.

"Thanks. I will!" Her mom called from the living room, and a second later Lacey heard the front door slam, and the house was silent.

She finished her math, then rolled over

on her back and stared at her bedroom ceiling, letting her mind drift over the events of the past week.

It was funny. She'd been focused on her unhappiness and bad luck for so long that she hadn't realized that a lot of good things had been happening to her. She'd been voted chairperson of an important committee in one of the most popular clubs in the school. Her posters were a huge success, so much so that the president of the French Club had contacted her about doing posters for their events. One of the prettiest, most popular girls in the school considered her a friend. There were lots of positive things happening in her life, and she had completely ignored them and instead had dwelled on the negative things. That was what had made her lose her best friend and her boyfriend.

She sighed. Tomorrow was Friday, the beginning of the weekend—only this weekend there would be no Kevin and Peg. She rolled off her bed and grabbed her poster-making materials. *I'll work on posters and watch TV until bedtime. Then tomorrow I'll apologize to Peg and wish her well with Kevin.*

She'd just finished the lettering on a brightly colored poster when she heard the front door creak open. She looked up to see Bill coming into the living room, juggling two large boxes in his arms. "Hi Lacey." He smiled at her pleasantly. "Your mom said it would be okay for me to bring a load of things over this evening."

"She told me you might bring some stuff over," Lacey said, rising to her feet. "Here, let me help you with those," she said, taking the smaller of the two boxes out of his arms.

"Thanks."

"Where does this stuff go?" Lacey asked.

"Your mom said for me to stack the boxed stuff in her bedroom and we'll sort through them this weekend."

Lacey nodded and led him into her mother's large bedroom, where they stacked the boxes in a corner.

"Are there more in your car?" Lacey asked.

"Well . . . yes, but I can manage," Bill replied.

"I don't mind helping. I really wasn't doing anything anyway." She knew she had surprised him by her generosity, but she had promised herself she would give him a chance and try to accept him as part of her life.

Together she and Bill walked out to his car. He opened the trunk, revealing a vast amount of fishing equipment and old gardening tools.

"Maybe we should put this stuff in the garage," Lacey suggested.

"Great idea," Bill agreed with a quick smile.

For the next few minutes they made several trips back and forth from the car trunk to the garage, storing Bill's things on one side.

"Your mother told me that you offered to be her maid of honor in the wedding," Bill finally said, breaking the silence. "I just wanted you to know that you made her very happy."

Lacey shrugged and untangled two fishing poles from each other. "I guess I did some growing up in the past few days," she answered softly.

Bill walked over and stood next to her. "Sometimes growing up can be incredibly hard."

Lacey thought of Peg and Kevin and nodded. "That's the understatement of the year!"

"Unfortunately, sometimes that growing-up process happens even when you're forty years old," he commented with a small laugh.

Lacey looked up at him curiously. "What do you mean?"

"I mean that I've had to do some painful growing up myself over the past few weeks," Bill explained.

Lacey looked at him in surprise. She'd never dreamed that adults went through any sort of growing-up process. She'd always thought that once people were grown up, they were . . . grown up! "What kind?" she asked curiously, leaning against the car and staring at him.

"Well, when your mom and I started to talk about getting married, I never gave much thought as to how you would feel about the marriage. I just assumed that automatically we'd be an instant family and live happily ever after." He smiled at her. "I've come to realize that was a very unrealistic way of looking at things."

Lacey blushed, slightly embarrassed as she thought of the many times she'd ignored him when he'd come to visit, how many times she'd been cold to him and snubbed him when he'd spoken to her.

"Anyway," Bill continued, "I want you to know that I know you had a real father, a man you loved very much, and I'll never try to take his place with you, but I think it would be nice if you and I could be friends."

"I'd like that," Lacey murmured with a small smile.

"Shall we shake on it?" Bill asked, holding out his hand to her. Lacey took his hand and shook it as he continued. "I don't really know too much about teenage girls, and more than likely at one point or another, I'll do something to make you angry. But if you ever feel like I'm being unfair, you tell me and we'll work it out."

Lacey nodded with a grin. "Likewise," she said, then picked up the fishing poles thoughtfully. "Maybe you should hang on to these."

"Why?" Bill looked at her curiously.

Lacey smiled at him shyly. "You never know when we might decide to take a vacation to some lake and do a little fishing."

Chapter 15

Lacey sat in psychology class and stared at the open textbook on the desk in front of her. Peg was at her desk on the right side of the room, and Kevin was at his desk in front of her. When Lacey had walked into the room for class, they'd been hunched over Kevin's desk, whispering intently to each other. When they'd seen her, they'd quickly broken apart and gone to their respective desks. Did they think she didn't know about the two of them? Did they think they were being sneaky or something? She stared at Kevin's back, miserable that she'd been stupid enough to lose such a great guy.

When the bell rang, Lacey raced away from her desk, not wanting to see Kevin and

Peg together again. She'd just walked out of
the room when Kevin came up behind her
and grabbed her arm, a grim, determined
look on his handsome face.

"Lacey, we've got to talk," he said, not
letting go of her arm.

Lacey blushed, realizing he probably
wanted to explain to her how he'd fallen in
love with Peg. "Kevin, you don't owe me any
explanations," she said stiffly, wishing he'd
let go of her arm so she could leave.

He looked at her incredulously. "Well,
you're certainly right about that!" he said
indignantly. "If anything, I think you owe
me an explanation, and an apology!" He
released her arm, but Lacey didn't run.

"An apology for what?" Now, she looked at
him incredulously. After all, he was the one
who had fallen in love with her best friend.
What had she done to him that required an
apology?

"For ignoring me all week. For refusing to
talk to me and going out of your way to
avoid me since our date!"

"I didn't think there was any point in
talking to you," Lacey replied, her gaze not
meeting his. It was so painful to look at
him, to like him so much, and know her
feelings were not returned.

"What do you mean, there wasn't any

point in talking to me? I think we really needed to talk, especially after the way our date ended the other night." He paused a moment as a group of kids went by, looking at them curiously, then he moved closer to her. His closeness made her instantly conscious of the scent of his familiar cologne. She knew she'd never be able to smell that particular brand of cologne and not think of Kevin.

"All the more reason for us not to talk," Lacey replied. "Besides," she added, "every time I saw you all week, you looked pretty busy."

"Busy? What are you talking about?" Kevin's eyes darkened with confusion.

"Peg," Lacey said tightly, her emotions choking her throat.

"What about Peg?" Kevin looked at her, bewildered.

"You and Peg . . . the two of you were together all week . . . I don't blame you for falling for each other. . . ." She let her voice trail off.

A look of comprehension crossed Kevin's face and he threw back his head and started laughing.

Lacey stared impatiently at him. "What's so funny?" she demanded, hurt that he was actually laughing at her.

"You mean you actually thought that Peg . . . and I . . ." He broke off and went into another fit of laughter. "I'm sorry," he gasped, taking a deep breath to get himself under control. His brown eyes were twinkling warmly as he grinned at her. "Lacey, Peg and I aren't interested in each other. The only thing Peg and I have in common is that we both care about you, and you've been driving us both crazy!"

Lacey stared at him. Was it possible that Kevin still liked her? Was it possible that it wasn't too late after all?

"Kevin—"

"Lacey—"

They spoke at the same time, then laughed self-consciously.

"You go first," Kevin said.

Lacey shook her head. "No, you first," she protested.

Kevin looked at her seriously. "Lacey, I do owe you an apology. I should never have butted into your personal life—you know, all that stuff about your mom and Bill. It wasn't any of my business, and I should have kept my big mouth shut."

Lacey shook her head. "No, it's my fault. I was having a great time on our date until I saw my mom and Bill at the theater, and I let them being there ruin the whole night

with you." Her face colored with embarrassment. "Then, you started talking about
them getting married, and I felt like you
were on my mom's side and not on my side,
and that made me so mad."

"Are you still mad at me?" He gazed
intently at her with his beautiful brown
eyes.

She smiled at him and shook her head.
"No, I'm sort of glad we had the fight. You
made me realize a lot of things."

Kevin grinned at her. "Lacey, I don't care
if you hate Bill. I just don't want any of that
to ruin things between us." He touched her
lightly on the shoulder. "Could we start all
over again? Would you go out with me again
tonight? We could go get a pizza or something." He looked at her hopefully.

Lacey hesitated. "I've got to work on some
posters tonight," she said, then brightened.
"But it you don't mind me working, you
could come over. We could watch TV or
something."

Kevin grinned. "That sounds great! What
time?"

"About eight o'clock?"

"Great!" He smiled at her for a minute
longer, then jumped as the warning bell
rang. "Oh, I gotta go. Coach is going to skin
me for being late. I'll see you tonight."

Lacey watched him go. Then, smiling dreamily, she slowly turned and began walking toward the lunchroom.

"Well, you've got that dopey look on your face again. I guess that means everything is all right between you and Kevin."

Lacey turned to see Peg leaning against the wall, obviously waiting for her. "Peg . . . I . . . I'm sorry," she began to apologize.

"Me, too." Peg smiled, then waved her hands to dismiss the subject. "Let's go get some lunch. Matchmaking always makes me hungry." She fell into step beside Lacey. "And remind me, sometime I'm going to make us each a list of ways to avoid having fights with best friends!"

By seven-thirty that evening, Lacey was ready and waiting for Kevin to arrive. She went into the kitchen and checked on the rice cereal and marshmallow snacks she'd made earlier. She hoped they would be good. She'd added extra marshmallows to make sure they were especially sweet.

She went back into the living room and began pacing the floor. Her stomach jumped with nervous tension, but it wasn't the same sort of nervousness she'd felt before her very first date with Kevin. All she could think about was the fact that he had told her he cared about her, that he wanted to see her again. Lacey hugged herself with delight, then jumped as the doorbell rang.

Lacey opened the front door, feeling her breath catch in her throat. Oh, Kevin was so handsome! Would she always feel so breathless when she saw him?

"Hi," he said with that funny, half-crooked smile that made Lacey's heart beat faster.

"Hi." Lacey smiled at him.

"Uh . . . can I come in?" His grin widened as Lacey blushed and led him into the living room.

"I'm sorry I've got to do all this work while you're here, but I promised the French club president I'd have five posters ready for her to pick up tomorrow morning," she explained as she led him around the paper and pens scattered around the living room floor. "They're having a fund-raiser and want to get the posters up immediately." She sat down on the floor and gestured for him to have a seat on the sofa.

Instead, he sat down on the floor next to her. "That's okay, I don't mind." He looked curiously at the two posters she'd already completed. "Wow! Did you do these? These are really great!"

She nodded, feeling a warm glow of pride.

"Gosh, Lacey, these are really beautiful!" He looked at her with admiration.

"Would you like me to turn on the television? I think there's a football game on," Lacey suggested.

"That would be great, if you don't mind." He grinned at her. "It's a college game, but it should be a good one, Miami against Oklahoma."

Lacey shrugged her shoulders. "I don't know anything about football," she admitted.

Kevin smiled at her. "You know, that's one thing I really like about you. You're honest. That day we all played football in the park, you didn't pretend to know the game like a lot of girls do. Besides," he teased her, "you're the only person I know who knows how to stop a football with your nose."

Lacey laughed and rubbed her nose ruefully. "Yeah, but it's not something I'd like to do every day."

"I'll tell you what. I'll explain what's happening in the football game if you'll teach me how to write my name like this."

"It's a deal!" Lacey smiled back at him.

For a minute they simply sat there and smiled at each other. Then Kevin slowly moved his head closer to her, and Lacey realized he was going to kiss her. Her heart fluttered wildly in her chest. Finally, she was going to get her first real kiss! She closed her eyes, but at the moment his lips were about to touch hers, the telephone rang shrilly, making them both jump apart.

"Hello!" Lacey practically yelled into the phone, frustrated because the moment of her first kiss had been ruined.

"May I speak to Susan?" an unfamiliar voice said at the other end of the line.

Lacey groaned inwardly. It was just her dumb luck! Her very first kiss had been spoiled by a wrong number! "I'm sorry, but you have the wrong number." Lacey hung up and smiled at Kevin. "Sorry," she murmured, wishing they could go back to where they had been before the telephone rang. "Uh . . . before I get started working, would you like a soda or something?"

"Sure," Kevin answered. "A soda would be great."

Lacey went into the kitchen and fixed two glasses of cola, then began cutting the pan of marshmallow bars into little squares. She got a small serving platter from one of the cabinets and began transferring the snacks from the pan to the platter. She frowned as the sticky snacks clung to her fingers. "Oh, great," she muttered, managing to get little squares stuck to both hands.

"Is there anything I can do to help?"

Lacey whirled around with her hands behind her back at the sound of Kevin's voice. "Uh . . . no . . ." A heated blush crept up Lacey's neck. That old, sick feeling began to grow in the pit of her stomach. Lacey's Law of bad luck was going to ruin everything! "I was just . . . uh . . . I made some . . ." She let her voice trail off with embarrassment.

She pulled her hands out from behind her back and looked at him helplessly. As their eyes met, his smile appeared at one corner of his lips, then slowly spread over his entire mouth. As Lacey saw his gorgeous smile, she realized it wasn't a disaster after all. In fact, it was funny. Wonderfully, tremendously funny! She burst out laughing, and Kevin joined right in. The more they looked at Lacey's hands with the rice-cereal squares hanging off them, the more hysterically they laughed. Lacey leaned back against the cabinets, weak with laughter. Her giggles caught in her throat as she found herself suddenly held firmly in Kevin's strong arms.

"I think it was my lucky day when you

tripped and nearly fell into my lap on the first day of school," he murmured.

Lacey blushed and looked up at him, awkwardly keeping her sticky hands away from him. "Why was it your lucky day?" she asked softly, intensely aware of his lips only inches away from hers.

"Because the day you fell on me, I think that was the day I began falling for you." His warm, gold-flecked, chocolate-colored eyes gazed at her, and then he slowly brought his lips down to meet hers in a tender, sweet kiss. Lacey closed her eyes, swept away by the warmth of his kiss, the frantic beating of her heart, and the beauty of the moment of her very first kiss.

When the kiss was over, Kevin took one of her hands and raised it to his lips, and bit off one of the sticky snacks that hung from her fingers. "These are really good," he said, and together they dissolved into another fit of giggles.

Lacey smiled. Never again would she think of her law as Lacey's Law of bad luck. From now on, it was going to be Lacey's Law of love!

Here's a sneak preview of *The Perfect Couple*, book number four in the continuing FIRST KISS series from Bantam Books:

"We're really good friends, aren't we, Mitch?"

As he turned to look at me, he pushed a tumble of rust-red hair back from his forehead. "What's on your mind, Dreyer?" he asked.

This was a lot harder than I'd thought it would be, and for a minute I wanted to tell him there was nothing on my mind, I was just making conversation. But he knew me too well for that. I could fool my parents some of the time, but I couldn't fool Mitch any of the time. He *knew* I had something to say, and he wouldn't let me off the hook until I told him what it was.

I gulped air the way I'd just gulped my soda, and then I got it out. "Starting on

Monday I want you to pretend to be my boyfriend!"

He chuckled. "What do you want us to do—put on a play in the garage? Don't you think we're a little too old for that?"

I'd never felt self-conscious with Mitch before, but now it was all I could do to look into his eyes. My voice was wobbly as I said, "It's nothing like that. But I do need your help, Mitch."

His smile was reassuring. "Just tell me what I can do for you. We're the Two Musketeers—right?"

"What I want us to be is Romeo and Juliet!" I burst out, grateful for the cue he'd thrown me. "And I don't mean for a play. I want us to start going together like a couple. You know—as if we were dating, and sort of in love."

Mitch gaped at me, his mouth almost as wide open as his eyes. "But—why?" he croaked.

I swallowed. This was getting harder by the minute, but somehow I managed to say, "Because I'm in love with Ty Rogers, and he won't notice me if I keep going around with other girls. All you have to do—"

That was as far as I got before Mitch bounded to his feet, his eyes shooting green sparks. "Are you out of your mind?" he yelped. "You want me to go out with you because you're in love with Ty Rogers? What kind of sense does that make?" Before I could try to explain he spat out, "Ty Rogers!" as if it had just got through to him who I was talking about. "I didn't think you even knew that guy was alive!"

I jumped up, too. "It's the other way around!" I flung back at him. "Ty doesn't know *I'm* alive." I knew I had no right to be angry with Mitch, but I was so disappointed that he was letting me down I had to get mad or cry—and I hadn't cried since I was a kid, except at the movies, which didn't count.

"That's good," Mitch growled, although he'd simmered down a little bit. "Quite a few girls at Bayside would be better off if that guy *hadn't* noticed they were alive." He paused, then said, "Ty Rogers!" for the third time. Each time he said the name he sounded more disgusted. "I don't know what you see in that showboat." He shook his head as if he were giving up on me.

Whether I had a right to be or not, I was suddenly furious with him. "I see that he's the handsomest, most exciting boy in school, and I'm going to attract his attention if I have to throw myself in front of his brother's car!" I yelled. I straightened up my bike and started to climb on. My eyes were blurred with tears, and I hardly knew what I was doing. To me, a friend was a friend and you helped him out, no matter how you felt about what he wanted to do.

"Hey, where are you going, Denny?" he hollered after me as I started to push off down the hill. In a few strides he'd caught up with me. "You didn't mean that about throwing yourself under Hank Rogers's car, did you?" He bent over, anxiously studying my face.

I'd never been able to stay mad at Mitch for more than a few minutes. "No, of course not," I said. "I guess I was just doing what Daddy calls my Bette Davis act." I smiled, but then without warning my eyes filled with tears again, and before I could blink them back, two big fat ones ran down my cheeks.

"You're crying!" Mitch gasped.

"I am not!" I couldn't help sniffling, though. It wasn't like me to be weepy and emotional, but I supposed that came from being in love. And Mitch wasn't going to help me, so Ty would never notice me. Never.

"You are, too," Mitch insisted gently. For a minute he looked helpless and bewildered. Then all at once he thrust out his jaw.

"We're going to sit down and talk this over." He pulled me off the bike, and wheeled it back where it had been. I followed, dragging my feet. I still didn't think he was going to help me. When we'd sat down on the bank again he said, "Exactly what do you want me to do, Denny? You know I'll help you if I can. You just caught me by surprise when you said—well, you know."

I was so choked up that Mitch wasn't letting me down, after all, that I couldn't speak right away. Then I remembered how important this was, and I repeated what I'd said about wanting to attract Ty's attention. "And he'll never look at me unless I'm going with another boy," I concluded.

Mitch frowned. "Why would he be interested in you because you're going with another guy? I'd feel the opposite way—that a girl was off-limits if she was going with someone else."

I could see where Mitch would feel that way, but Ty was more competitive . . . which might be the reason he was a star quarterback while Mitch was only the back-up.

"That just happens to be the way Ty is," I said. "I've been watching him for three weeks now, and he simply doesn't glance at a girl who's alone, or with other girls."

Mitch made a grunting sound that wasn't really a word. Then he said, "So you want us to pretend we're—in love."

"Sort of," I replied. "We'll hang out together around school, and go to The Last Straw together, and maybe the movies."

Mitch picked up a handful of dirt and let it run through his fingers while he mulled the whole thing over. Mitch never rushed into things, but once he'd made up his mind to do something you could count on him to see it through to the end.

After what seemed like hours, Mitch looked at me. "There's just one problem I see in all this," he said. "What if I should get interested in another girl? I couldn't ask her out if she thought I was dating you."

"Another girl?" I gasped. For some reason I was stunned by the idea.

"Yeah. I didn't tell you, but a while ago I thought I was in love with Patty McDougal. I'm over it now, but it could happen again at any time."

"Patty McDougal!" I said as it suddenly got through to me who he'd been talking about. She had about a thousand freckles, and she still hadn't lost all her baby fat. I didn't want to put her down to Mitch, though, so I said, "She's—real pretty."

"Yeah, I guess," Mitch said, "but she

giggles too much. I began to notice it after a while, and it got on my nerves."

"Do I giggle too much?" I asked, suddenly anxious.

"You don't giggle, exactly," he said. "When you laugh it sounds kind of like my mother's music box. Tinkling, you know."

I was so relieved I did giggle, and then we both burst out laughing. Finally I remembered how serious this was, and I told Mitch that if he got interested in another girl we'd just pretend to break up. "The same way we will if—when—Ty gets interested in me."

Mitch wrapped his arms around his knees and looked off across the road. Finally he straightened up and looked at me. "I don't know about that guy, Denny. I'd hate to see you hurt, and the way he goes from one girl to another—"

"That's because he hasn't met the right girl yet," I interrupted.

"And you think you're the right girl for him?"

"Don't you think I'm pretty enough for him to like me?" I said. Mitch was a boy, too. Maybe he knew I didn't have a chance with Ty, or any other attractive guy.

He held out his hands in a helpless gesture. "Gosh, I have no idea of how you look to other guys, Denny. That would be like me trying to guess how my sister looks to those little twerps in her eighth-grade class. You're just Denny to me."

"Yeah, I know," I mumbled. "The same way you're just Mitch to me."

We were both silent for a while, then Mitch said, "I've got a couple of candy bars. Let's eat them to seal our bargain."

"Then we have a bargain? You're going to help me out?"

"Sure. We go into action Monday morning. That's what you want, isn't it?"

"Oh, Mitch!" I threw my arms around his neck, as a big bubble of excitement burst inside me. "You're the best friend anyone ever had!"